Michelle Smart's love affair with books started when she was a baby and would cuddle them in her cot. A voracious reader of all genres, she found her love of romance established when she stumbled across her first Mills & Boon book at the age of twelve. She's been reading them—and writing them—ever since. Michelle lives in Northamptonshire, England, with her husband and two young Smarties.

CLAIMING HIS BABY AT THE ALTAR

MICHELLE SMART

MILLS & BOON

First published in Great Britain 2022
by Mills & Boon, an imprint of HarperCollins*Publishers* Ltd,
1 London Bridge Street, London, SE1 9GF

www.harpercollins.co.uk

HarperCollins*Publishers*
1st Floor, Watermarque Building,
Ringsend Road, Dublin 4, Ireland

Large Print edition 2022

Claiming His Baby at the Altar © 2022 Michelle Smart

ISBN: 978-0-263-29548-1

08/22

CHAPTER ONE

THE FLASH OF cameras was blinding.

Flora Hillier kept her gaze fixed ahead and ignored the questions being shouted at her by the horde of jostling reporters. A microphone brushed against her cheek. Another jabbed her neck. She would not give the vultures the satisfaction of reacting.

The dozen or so steps she climbed to enter the centuries-old building were wide but short in depth and she prayed not to trip.

At the top of the steps, the double doors were opened for her. A court guard took her arm and swept her inside.

The low-level hum of noise inside the court building was a welcome contrast to the shouts and hollers she'd just endured. Flora removed her sunglasses and placed a hand to her aching lower back. The pain had been strong enough to wake her that morning.

Filling her lungs with air and fortitude, she

put her bag on the tray to be scanned and stepped through the body scanner. She wondered if this level of security had long been a part of Monte Cleure's criminal court or if they'd installed it specially for Ramos. She imagined there were any number of people out there who would be happy to form an orderly queue for the opportunity to do harm to the Spanish bastard. She'd be right at the front of it.

He was here, in this building. Soon, very soon, she would see him again. More importantly, he would see her.

She approached the curved reception area and handed her passport over.

The lady checking it raised an arched eyebrow before inputting the details into a desktop computer. 'Look in the camera,' she said in English, pointing up.

Flora lifted her stare to the domed device on the ceiling. Less than a minute later, a lanyard pass with her name and picture was handed to her.

'Go to room four,' the lady ordered.

'Thank you.'

Sliding the lanyard over her head, Flora

headed down the wide corridor until she found the room.

Justin was already there, huddled around an oval table with his small legal team. He greeted her with an exhausted smile.

She held up a sympathetic hand to him and then sank gratefully onto a chair one of the legal team pulled out for her, and rubbed again at her aching lower back.

Today was the start of a trial expected to last two weeks. When found guilty, Justin could expect to spend two decades behind bars.

Monte Cleure allowed reduced time for good behaviour only in the most exceptional circumstances. Funnily enough, those exceptional circumstances only ever seemed to apply to the fabulously rich. Justin was no longer rich. Ramos had made sure of that. Ramos had also made sure the evidence against Justin was watertight. Ramos had chosen Monte Cleure to press charges against him deliberately.

It pained Flora beyond reason that the case against Justin was watertight only because Justin was guilty of the crimes he was about to go on trial for. Theft of a million euros. Fraud had been added to the charge for good measure.

Which room was Ramos currently holed up in? The one next door? Further away? No doubt he too would be huddled around a table with his legal team. Maybe two tables to fit them all in. His team would vastly outnumber Justin's. What was the atmosphere like in that room? She doubted it was the resigned, subdued atmosphere permeating this one. Most likely, anticipation and expectation.

Anticipation and expectation that Justin Hillier be not only punished but destroyed.

If Flora had any tears left in her she would weep for her brother but the last year had spent her of them. There came a time when they would no longer form. Her tear ducts had simply dried up.

A knock echoed on the door. An official stepped in.

It was time.

Flora heaved herself back to her weary feet and stared into her brother's gaunt face. She straightened his tie even though it was already perfect, wiped away a fleck of imaginary flint from the lapel of his suit jacket, and kissed his cheek.

'I love you,' she whispered to the man who'd been more of a father to her than theirs had ever been.

His smile was sad. 'I love you too.'

There was nothing more to be said.

The hum of noise when Flora had arrived was now a buzz, the corridor bustling with bodies. It was a rare event that Monte Cleure's criminal court was the setting for such a high-profile crime. The principality was used to the press swarming for the goings-on of its rotten royal family and the fabulously wealthy people who inhabited the glamorous, sunlit place, and when Flora was led to the front of the public gallery overlooking the court, the press were already crammed into their section like eager expectant meerkats, faces bobbing in all directions for the star attraction's appearance.

They didn't have to wait long.

The prosecution team entered. Amongst them strode the tall figure of Alejandro Ramos, suave and gorgeous in a navy suit and tie and grey shirt. Today, he was clean shaven, his thick dark hair cropped short.

The last thing Flora expected was the jump of her heart into her throat at his appearance.

She placed her trembling hands on her belly and breathed deeply, telling herself the jump of her heart was only to be expected considering the last time she'd seen him had been when he'd passionately kissed her goodbye.

Much better was the spike of hatred that came when he sat amongst the prosecution lawyers on the prosecution bench. The spike pierced her to see him as one with them. In England he'd be nothing more than a witness.

Look at me, she silently urged him.

The smooth-looking man seated beside him whispered in his ear. Ramos tilted his head to hear more clearly then nodded with a grin.

How could he smile when he was condemning his best friend to decades of imprisonment?

Look at me.

The Justice of the Peace entered the court from his private room at the back.

An order was called out. Everyone rose to their feet.

The Justice took his seat and indicated for everyone to follow suit.

Flora, her stare fixed on Ramos, stayed standing.

Look at me, you bastard.

As if he could feel the weight of her stare, he turned his face up to the gallery. To her.

Flora had chosen her clothing that morning with care. She'd selected a simple, short-sleeved cream summer dress with tiny buttons running its length that fitted snugly over her form. She'd wanted nothing that could detract the eye from the huge swelling of her stomach.

For the briefest of moments Ramos's eyes locked on hers then flittered away as if he hadn't seen her.

A wave of longing crashed through her, as unexpected and as frightening as the jump in her heart at the sight of him had been, but she swallowed hard and remained standing.

Barely a beat passed when she caught the sudden stillness in his frame.

Slowly, he turned his gaze back up to her.

Clenching her teeth tightly in an attempt to keep any emotion from showing on her face, Flora pointed both forefingers at her belly.

If he was looking closely enough he would see the bulge where their child had just kicked her.

If the situation weren't so desperate and heartbreaking, Flora would have found much amusement in the first hour of the trial. The leading prosecutor rose and made his opening speech, not a word of which she understood as it was all conducted in French. Ramos would have understood but she was willing to bet not a single word penetrated his head.

The supremely confident, arrogant man who'd walked into the courtroom looked shell-shocked. Poor diddums. Her heart bled for him. It really did.

Only when the prosecutor sat back down did any animation show on his handsome face, and he whispered into the ear of the man beside him, who in turn whispered down the line until the whispers reached the prosecutor, who got back up and shuffled over to Ramos. The pair of them whispered frantically between themselves. The whispering culminated in Ramos scrawling onto a piece of paper that was immediately handed to the Justice, who read it, rose to his feet, addressed the court, and then swept back into his room.

The buzz in the courtroom as everyone filed out was strong enough for Flora to feel it on her skin. The excitement coming from the press box and the many glances being thrown her way told Flora her stunt hadn't gone unnoticed. It couldn't be helped. She'd tried everything else.

Rather than join the exodus, she stayed seated and closed her eyes. The muscles on her face hurt from the tight, unmoving position she'd held them in and, now that she relaxed them, emotions she'd contained just as tightly rose to the surface and threatened to choke her.

Rubbing her belly, she concentrated on breathing in and out. Something was going to happen and she needed to be calm and in her zen zone to cope with whatever that something would be.

Would Ramos decide to ignore her obvious pregnancy just as he'd successfully ignored her these last eight months? Ignore was the wrong word. He hadn't ignored her. He'd ghosted her. He'd seduced her, kissed her *adios* and then cut her dead.

Or would he acknowledge her pregnancy but think it a jest? Or assume another man was the father?

She would put nothing past him.

If he ignored her or denied paternity then so be it. She was mentally prepared for that. She had the trial to get through and she needed to stay strong for Justin's sake.

She'd done her duty and ensured her baby's daddy knew their child existed. The rest was up to him. For Flora, best case scenario would be Ramos acknowledged their child, offered child support—she really didn't want to have to go the legal route for that—and limited his involvement to the odd visitation. He wouldn't want to be a full-time father, that was for sure, not with his lifestyle. A baby would definitely cramp his style.

'*Mademoiselle?*'

She opened her eyes.

An official beckoned her.

She summoned a smile and heaved herself to her feet. She hadn't realised how exhausted she was until she put one foot in front of the other. That silent confrontation with Ramos had drained her. She supposed it was because it had been so long in coming and she'd built it up so much in her head. The ache in her back felt more intense.

As she left the viewing gallery, she was about to head to her brother's designated room when the official touched her arm and pointed in the other direction.

'*Mademoiselle?* Come.'

Immediately pulled out of the zen zone she'd calmed herself into, Flora hesitated before following.

Okay, so it looked as if Ramos wasn't going to ignore her.

The official pushed a door open. It was a waiting room with a coffee machine and plump sofas and, though she'd expected to find him there, her heart still leapt back up her throat.

He was sitting on a single sofa, leaning forwards, hands locked together.

His dark brown eyes penetrated her from the first lock of their gazes.

Flora had imagined this moment so many times. She'd planned how she would act and what she would say. Act nonchalant. Speak only in practical terms about their child. Do not do or say anything that would make him think she felt anything for him but contempt.

The reality was very different. Enough emotions zoomed through her to make her nauseous with their strength. Hate. Fury. Despair. Longing. The last of them was the worst.

How could she long for him after the way he'd treated her?

How could she have fallen under his spell in the first place?

Flora had known Ramos since she was eleven years old and he and Justin eighteen-year-old students. The young Spanish man had been a regular presence in the Hillier home. He'd even joined them for Christmas a couple of times.

Her brother's closest friend, a veritable hunk in impeccably tailored clothing, a classically chiselled handsome face women swooned over...and, boy, didn't he know it. Flora had been determined not to become one of those swooners. The way Ramos and her brother treated women had nauseated her. They might as well have set up a deli counter and handed out numbers to the 'lucky' recipients who would be discarded in turn before they got stale.

Ramos had discarded Flora even quicker than he'd discarded the others.

His set jaw loosened enough for him to say, 'You should sit.'

Thirteen years she'd known him. That his lightly accented voice had a real depth and richness to it were qualities she'd only noticed the night they spent together.

Now, it fell like velvet on her ears and it shook her enough for her to force a laugh to cover it. 'That's the first thing you have to say to me? *You should sit?*'

'You look like you're about to collapse.'

Aww, he was concerned about her welfare. Such generosity of spirit.

Easing herself carefully onto a leather two-seater, she wished her huge size hadn't made her movements so ungainly and graceless when every inch of him reeked of sophistication. It was just another of the discrepancies between them, all weighted in his favour.

Until today, she'd rather enjoyed being so obviously pregnant. The number of smiles she would see as people clocked her watermelon belly lightened her heart. There was something magical about the late stage of pregnancy that people responded to and she liked that it made her feel less alone in a world where her mother was dead, her father an unreliable, useless deadbeat and her beloved brother incarcerated.

Now she felt none of the magic, only a weight in her chest that her precious child should be saddled with such an unworthy and undeserving father.

Ramos's full but firm lips were tightly compressed as his uncompromising gaze scrutinised every inch of her. He really did have beautiful eyes, so dark they could be mistaken for black, and with such depth that a woman could lose herself in them.

Flora had avoided looking into those eyes for years and a pang ripped through her heart to remember the night they had gazed at her with such intensity and then melted with something more than naked desire, something that had filled every cavity in her chest and seen her fall into their hypnotic pull.

'When is the child due?' he asked.

She blinked the unwelcome memory away and forced her voice to remain steady. 'In three weeks.'

He exhaled and inclined his head. 'I am to assume from your stunt in the courtroom that it is mine?'

'Yes.'

If he asked how she knew it was his, she would throw her bag at him.

'And I am to assume that your stunt was designed to bring attention to this to the whole world?'

Her mouth dropped open. Incredulous, she shook her head and laughed. 'Seriously?'

His jaw clenched again. 'What else am I

supposed to think? A note to a member of my legal team would have been as effective.'

'I would have done that if I thought you'd read it.' She wished she could sit straight with ease and cross her legs, project the image she wanted him to see rather than the reality, which included swollen feet and ankles. Instead, she had to use her elbows for purchase to straighten. 'I've spent seven months trying to tell you.'

He raised a sceptical eyebrow.

Quelling the burst of fury this provoked and determined to speak without a hint of emotion, Flora leaned forwards as much as her belly would allow and eyeballed him. 'You blocked my phone number and email. I called two of your homes and spoke to two of your housekeepers. I spoke to your PA three times. I wrote you four letters. *Four.* I told you in every single one of those letters and the messages I left for you that I was pregnant with your child, but it wasn't until I made another call to your office and spoke to a temp that I was told you had instructed all communications from me in whatever form they came to be ignored or destroyed and that anyone who so much as whispered my name to you would be fired for gross misconduct. You cut me off dead and refused to have my name spoken in front of you, not just a refusal but a specific order—*that's* why I had to show you publicly. It was the only way to guarantee you'd notice.'

Ramos's hands were still clasped together but now the knuckles had whitened. The tension on his handsome face was such that the flick of a pebble onto it would see it shatter.

Low in Flora's belly, her baby shifted. It was a movement she adored, and had the effect of staunching the anger that had been building in her. She rubbed in big, sweeping motions and was rewarded with a foot or a hand poking against her palm.

She didn't want to get angry and lose her temper. Trying to maintain a zen edge for her baby's sake while her life was falling apart at the seams had, at times, felt impossible, but from the moment the pink line appeared on the pregnancy stick, protective love for her growing baby had overridden all the other emotions engulfing her. That love was primal, strong enough to douse the terror of a future raising a child alone without the mother she'd loved with all her heart and the brother who—for all his faults in his personal life—had always been there for her; a rock for her to lean on. Flora had found an inner strength she'd never known she had and she was not going to let Ramos undo all that hard work, especially not so close to the birth.

But it was so hard. Being in the same room as him for the first time in eight months was awakening memories she'd spent eight months trying her best to forget...

Waking in his arms, their mouths fusing together and then the fusion of their bodies before Ramos woke enough to drag himself away for protection...that memory came in a rush of vivid colour. The passion she'd experienced with him, the utter rightness she'd felt in his arms.

She pulled the strap of her bag over her shoulder. If the pain in her back hadn't sharpened, she would have hauled herself to her feet. She wanted out of this room and away from the man who'd taken her to heaven and dropped her into hell.

'Well, you know about the baby now,' she said, speaking tightly through the pain. 'Let's get this trial over and done with and then we can talk about your future involvement.'

He leaned his muscular body forward, animation returning to his eyes, his movements like those human statues she'd seen on the Embankment and Trafalgar Square. 'Future involvement?'

'If you want to be a part of his or her life…' She pinched the bridge of her nose, knowing he would likely want no involvement at all. 'Entirely up to you, but I will need child support. The sooner the better.'

Distaste flashed on his face. 'So that's what that little scene was all about. You're after my money.'

Flora clenched her teeth and swallowed back a fresh wave of anger. 'You're the father. You had a right to know, but your insistence on having Justin tried in a country where every criminal trial is prosecuted whether or not the defendant pleads guilty has wiped me out financially.'

The clenching of his jaw was pronounced. '*Someone* had to help him.' The pain had lessened enough for Flora to straighten her back, the act of straightening her spine injecting another dose of steel into it. 'You chose to prosecute him in a country that doesn't have legal aid and made sure all his assets were frozen. Well, *I* paid for his legal fees, by remortgaging my home and taking a loan on my business and I am now skint, so yes, I want your money, as much as the law entitles me to but only so I don't have to raise our child in poverty, and if you want to think me a gold-digger for that then be my guest. I couldn't give a fig what you think of me. I care about two things—my brother and my child. You've already ruined my brother and I will not let you ruin my child too, and if you want to fight me about money then fine, when the press next swarm around me, I will talk to them and I will give a statement and I will tell the world how the father of my unborn child seduced me when I went to him pleading for mercy and then cut me dead, and I will name and shame you.'

His bronzed skin darkened with every word she said, a tight contortion of emotions playing on his face. And then he smiled.

It was the cruellest smile she'd ever seen. 'Will you tell them how you prostituted yourself too?'

CHAPTER TWO

RAMOS'S ICILY DELIVERED words hit Flora like a slap.

A burning flush crawled up her neck and covered her face.

'You talk of me seducing you...?' He shook his head, the smile twisting. 'What a selective memory you have. Let me refresh it for you. *You* came to *me*. You shared a drink with me and while your mouth was pleading with me to show mercy to your brother, your big, beautiful, seductive brown eyes were eating me alive. You were as sweet and seductive as chocolate. A hot little *bombón*.'

His voice had developed into a cruel, silken caress.

'You leaned into me for that first kiss. You put your hand on my chest *right here*.' He put a hand to the spot. 'And then you touched my face.'

Flora covered her flaming cheeks and

squeezed her eyes tightly shut against the invading memories of the moment she'd finally fallen into the hypnotic spell of Ramos's eyes.

'You waited until we were both naked before you saw fit to mention that you were a virgin.' His laughter was bitter. 'You must really love your brother to sell your virginity like that.'

'It wasn't like that and you know it,' she whispered.

God help her, it had been *nothing* like that. It had just happened. One minute they'd been talking, the next...

No, she didn't want to remember that. Not that. Not the most thrilling, heady moment of her entire life.

Flora had spent years actively avoiding the Alejandro Ramos deli counter and then when she'd woken in his bed in the most delirious bubble of happiness, she'd been stupid enough to believe that what they'd shared had been so wonderful and beautiful that it had moved him as much as it had moved her.

For a few short hours she'd been stupid enough to believe that he felt something for her that went beyond sex.

An edge formed in his voice. 'Yes, *querida*, it was like that. You came to me with the implicit intention of seducing me into mercy and you so nearly got away with it.'

She snapped her eyes back open.

His top lip curled and he shook his head disparagingly. 'I read the message from him.'

'What message?' She didn't have a clue what he was on about.

'From your brother. In the morning. While you were sleeping. I went downstairs. I wanted to surprise you with breakfast in bed.' He shook his head again. 'Your bag had spilt over the coffee table.'

It had toppled when Ramos had lifted her into his arms to carry her upstairs to his bedroom and her foot had knocked the table. Her heart throbbed at the memory of it.

'The message flashed on your phone when I picked it up to put it in the bag for you. Do you remember what it said?'

Flora remembered little of that day. She'd been floating too high on her delirious Alejandro Ramos bubble of bliss for anything else to reach her.

The evening had been a different matter.

When she realised he'd deliberately stood her up, the bubble she'd been floating in had plummeted so hard and so fast the landing had bruised every part of her.

'It said, Any news, Flo? Did your charms work their magic on him?' He laughed, a horrid, bitter sound totally unlike his usual throaty laughter. His top lip curled again. 'I should have guessed when you turned up at my door dressed for seduction that Hillier had sent you.'

'I can't believe you've interpreted it that way,' she said hoarsely, her brain reeling. 'And Justin didn't send me. He knew what I was doing because I told him, but me coming to see you was *my* idea.'

Flora had driven her hire car from the Monte Cleure prison over the border into Spain and then on to Barcelona with her brother's gaunt face lodged in her retinas, desperately wondering what words she could say to make the notoriously unforgiving Alejandro Ramos show mercy to his best friend.

Justin deserved punishment, she knew that, but he needed help too.

Her brother had always been there for her:

the boy who humoured his baby sister when she demanded he play dolls with her, the young adolescent who walked her to school, made her packed lunches and helped with her homework when their mum was working, the adolescent who patiently taught her to play chess and made himself late for his school leavers party so they could finish a game of Scrabble, the young man who taught her how to drive and then forgave her when she reversed his precious car into a lamppost.

He'd always been there for her and she would always be there for him, even if the guilt and shame over what he'd done didn't hang over him like a shroud.

'Did your charms work their magic on him?' Ramos repeated the quote in a snarl, and for the first time Flora saw real anger rise to the surface.

'Do you really believe I traded my virginity to save my brother's skin?' The horror of it turned her blood to ice.

He just stared at her, only the tightening of his lips betraying his thoughts.

Dear heavens, he *did* believe it.

Ramos thought she'd gone to him with the

deliberate intention of exchanging her body for her brother's freedom.

Justin's message—his phone was the one thing the Monte Cleure prison authorities had allowed him to keep—had been a form of gallows humour she now remembered. He'd thought her mission to beg for Ramos's mercy a fool's errand.

Despair had her throw her arms in the air. 'I *never* expected what happened between us to happen. I came to you not knowing if you'd even open the door for me.'

'But I did open the door to you,' he said, unmoved. 'And *you* made the first move… you, who had always treated me with such disdain.' His nostrils flared, the anger that had slipped back beneath the handsome mask showing itself again. 'Whether you intended it to go as far as it did…' He inhaled deeply then shrugged, his large body relaxing. 'Play with fire, expect to be burned.'

'So that's why you ghosted me?' She was hardly able to form the words over the dizziness in her head.

She'd assumed it was because their night had either meant nothing to him or his hatred of her brother overrode any feelings he might have developed for her or because she'd been such a boring lover that he'd rather fire all his staff than see her again. Or a combination of all the above.

She'd been wrong on all counts. Ramos had ghosted her because he thought *she* had used *him*.

He hooked an ankle over a thigh, his voice returning to its normal velvety timbre. 'You tried to play me for a fool, what else did you expect?'

A fresh swell of pain in her lower back struck and all she could give in the way of denial was a hissed, 'I *didn't*.'

He raised another sceptical eyebrow and studied her with that intense scrutinising look that burned through her skin. She could practically feel him thinking what his next move would be, and when his handsome features loosened into a sardonic smile and he folded his arms across his chest, fearful anticipation of what came next had her holding her breath.

'It no longer matters,' he dismissed decisively. 'You came to me for your brother's freedom—I am sure this is not the way you thought you would gain it, not back then, but it has worked. Congratulations. I am willing to drop the charges against him…'

His words hanging between them, his smile widened. 'But to get that freedom for him, you will have to marry me.'

The room spun around her so quickly and so suddenly that Flora had to grip hard on the arm of the sofa to spot herself back into place.

Her vocal cords were paralysed.

Ramos laughed. A less bitter laugh but one that still landed like nails on a chalkboard. 'I see that I have shocked you into silence—that must be a first. But that's okay. You can thank me later.'

That unfroze her vocal cords! '*Thank* you?'

'Your brother gets his freedom and, as my wife, you will have access to more money than you could have dreamed of. I will have a prenuptial agreement drawn up, of course, but you will be very well provided for.' He flashed his teeth at her. 'See? I can be generous. Be nice to me and I can be *very* generous.'

She shook her head, utterly dumbfounded. 'I wouldn't marry you if you were the last man on earth.'

He shrugged as if he didn't care. 'If you want your brother to be freed you will.'

'But why, when you hate me so much?'

'I like to think of it as self-preservation.' His dark eyes glittered. 'Sometimes it is wise to keep your enemy close.'

'But...why marriage? Why something so drastic?'

Rising to his feet and removing his phone from the inside pocket of his suit jacket, he smiled as if she were a simpleton. 'Because, my little *bombón*, I know how much you hate me. I want you where I can keep an eye on you and make it impossible for you to keep our child from me and poison them against me. Now excuse me one moment. I need to update my legal team.'

With that, he strode to the other side of the room, turning his back on her at the same moment a sudden tightening down low in her abdomen sucked the air from her lungs.

Breathing hard until the cramping pain subsided, Flora tried her hardest to find her zen and kill the panic that was hitting her from all directions.

The abdominal pain she'd experienced was only a Braxton Hicks, she assured herself. She'd had a number of them in recent weeks. It was her body's way of preparing itself for the birth.

And Ramos was just playing with her. Punishing her some more for the crime he believed she'd committed of sleeping with him as a ruse to soften him to her brother's cause.

It devastated her to know he believed that of her, but it explained so much. If she had learned anything about Alejandro Ramos over the years it was that he held no forgiveness. He'd been cutting people—friends—who he considered to have abused his trust from his life without mercy and without hearing their defence long before Justin's betrayal.

In a minute he would tell her it had all been one big jest and then he would sweep out of the room and continue his destruction of the man who'd been his closest friend.

She could scarcely believe this was the same man who'd made love to her with such intense passion and awoken such intense passion in *her*.

Flora's feelings for Ramos had always been intense, from the minute he'd first walked into her childhood home with the swagger of someone who'd been a regular visitor his entire life.

He'd been eighteen years old, gregarious and gorgeous. She'd been eleven and resentful at having to share the precious time she had with her brother, who she'd missed terribly since he'd left for university. Her resentment grew when Ramos tagged along to many more of Justin's visits home and mushroomed at her brother's sycophantic behaviour.

If Ramos cracked a joke, Justin would laugh as if it was the funniest thing he'd ever heard. If Ramos gave an opinion on something, Justin would treat his words with the same respect he would an academic philosopher. Hillier and Ramos, they called each other, like something from a bad police television programme. Buddies on the university rugby pitch, drinking and pulling buddies off it. Sometimes they even remembered to study.

Resentment and jealousy turned markedly darker when she turned thirteen and went to stay with Justin for a weekend. By then, he'd moved into the six-bedroom house with its own basement games room that Ramos's billionaire father had bought his only child. He'd promised their mum that Ramos would be spending the weekend with his father in Barcelona and that it would be just him and Flora at the Oxford house. He'd spoil her rotten, taking her around Oxford's plentiful art shops and museums, and treating her to dinner at a posh restaurant. He'd even bought her a plethora of embroidery supplies. Even back then, Flora had a love of embroidery and a vague plan to turn her love into a career.

When she'd woken the next morning, she'd been sleepily opening her bedroom door when the door on the other side of the vast square hallway opened. She'd frozen on the spot.

Ramos had come out, laughing over his shoulder, leaned over and picked something off the floor then strode back in and closed the door behind him. He hadn't noticed his buddy's baby sister watching him.

He'd been naked.

The hot, sticky sensation that had flushed over and through her skin at the sight of his nude body, all muscular yet lean with a smattering of dark hair in the centre of his chest that ran down to his abdomen and tapered until it thickened at the place where his large *thing* was, had confused and disturbed her, and she'd hidden under her bed covers until Justin had come in to see if she was awake.

Later, after an awkward breakfast with Justin, Ramos and a pretty blonde woman wearing a dressing gown that was far too big for her, Flora had overheard Ramos apologise to Justin.

'Sorry, Hillier,' he'd said. 'Forgot your sister would be here. My father took a last-minute break to our villa in Martinique so I flew back and hooked up with Miranda. Sorry if she was too, err, vocal.'

She hadn't heard her brother's reply because the hot, sticky sensation had flushed through her again. She'd been growing up. She'd known exactly what Ramos had meant.

For over a decade, something about Alejandro Ramos had put her perpetually on edge and made her insides feel all swollen. Whatever those feelings were or meant, be they loathing or something more dangerous, she was now only weeks from giving birth to his child.

His smile was smug when he ended the call and strolled back to her. 'Good news,' he said, perching on the arm of the chair he'd been sitting on. 'We can marry right now.'

'You what?' she said dumbly.

'We can marry now… Well, in an hour. I've got the team drawing up the prenup for us, so we'll need to get that signed first, and sign a declaration that we are unencumbered and don't have other spouses hidden away, but other than that we are good to go.'

For the first time she realised he was actually being serious. 'But…we *can't*.'

'Monte Cleure law says we can. We both have our passports here. We will marry and then I will have all the charges dropped and your brother will be a free man.'

'Ramos, will you slow down a minute?' she begged. The room was starting to spin again.

'When you are my wife, you will call me Alejandro.'

'I've called you Ramos since my brother brought you home thirteen years ago.'

'You called me Alejandro the night we conceived our child,' he corrected silkily.

Heat filled her head to remember how she'd cried out his name when he'd brought her to her first ever climax, and she pressed her palm to her burning forehead to blot the memories away.

She sucked in a long breath. 'Are you really prepared to drop all the charges against Justin?'

'If you marry me, yes.'

'Can you do that?'

'Without me, there is no case. I will withdraw my testimony and all the evidence.'

'The prosecutor might still go ahead with it.'

'He won't.'

Frustration had her raise her voice for the first time. 'But how can you know?'

'You will just have to trust me.'

'Yeah, right. Get the charges dropped and then I'll marry you.'

'Do I look stupid?'

'I know you're not stupid, but it's the fairest way of going about it.'

'Possibly, but the sad fact is, my pretty little *bombón*, you are not to be trusted, so it's marriage first, charges dropped second or no deal. And if you think you can marry me and then divorce me as soon as your brother's set free then I warn you now, the charges will be slapped back on him and he will spend the best years of his life in a prison cell. There will be no divorce.'

As languid as a panther, he stepped to her and lowered his face. His spicy scent seeped into her airwaves and before his hypnotic stare could capture her, Flora closed her eyes tightly and held her breath.

He whispered, 'One hour, and then your nightmare will be over. Your brother will be free and you will have all the riches you could ever want.' He traced a finger lightly over her cheek.

His touch made her stiffen.

It also set her pulses surging.

All her nerves strained as his face moved closer. His breath whispered against the sensitive skin of her ear, sending tingles dancing through her.

'It looks like your selling of your soul to the devil has paid off,' he murmured. 'I congratulate you. Your brother will be very proud when you tell him how you bought his freedom.'

The air around her swirled as he walked away.

Flora kept her eyes tight shut until she heard the door close.

Once certain she was alone, she wrapped her arms around her belly and expelled the breath she'd held for so long, and tried to clear the fuzz in her head enough to think.

Thinking proved impossible. Her head was too full.

This was crazy.

How could he still affect her like this? It shouldn't be possible, not after everything he'd done.

But he thought she'd slept with him for her brother. He thought she'd used him…

There had been a moment—only a brief one—when she thought she'd seen hurt flash in his eyes.

Oh, this was all so confusing! As *if* she could have hurt him. The man had the hide of a rhino.

But even if she had and if he'd genuinely misinterpreted her brother's message, that didn't excuse him ghosting her, not after the night they'd shared, or from kissing her goodbye the way he had and making promises to see her he'd never had any intention of keeping.

If he'd genuinely believed that then why hadn't he confronted her about it? The answer to that came quickly—that was what Ramos did. Wrong him and he severed you from his life without thought or hesitation.

He *couldn't* mean to marry her.

Another tightening cramp low in her abdomen cut her panicked thoughts off sharply. Pressing a hand to the underside of her belly, frightened to find that her belly seemed to have sucked itself in and that she could feel the outline of her baby even more clearly, she gritted her teeth and breathed through her nose.

By the time it eased, her forehead was damp with perspiration.

How long had passed since the last one? Twenty minutes? More? Less?

She forced herself to think clearly and take note of the time. She'd had four Braxton Hicks total, each days apart. None had gone on as long as those two. None had been as painful.

Was her baby coming now? It couldn't be! It was too soon. She wasn't due for another three weeks.

Her back was aching again. It hadn't really stopped aching, just ebbed to a dull ache. It wasn't dull now.

Her tear ducts had started working again too. There was a hot sting in her eyes and she wished with all her heart that her mum were still here. She needed her desperately, for advice and comfort over the coming hours.

But her mother had been dead two years and there was no one else she could turn to for advice, at least no one whose advice she trusted, and, feeling more alone than she'd done since Justin's arrest, Flora began to rock lightly, backwards and forwards.

Marry Ramos and set Justin free.

Marry Ramos and—

'You are required to read and sign this, *mademoiselle.*'

Flora blinked. She hadn't noticed the door open.

The suited woman handed a document to her.

Flora cleared her throat. 'What is it?'

'For you to sign.'

'Helpful,' she muttered. She'd taken in only that it was a prenuptial agreement when the next contraction hit.

Her fingers tightened around the document but she gritted her teeth tightly and kept her gaze fixed on it, refusing to allow so much as a moan of pain leave her mouth.

'Are you okay, *mademoiselle*?'

She nodded and managed to make a noise that sounded a bit like *ahuh*. Once she'd ridden the pain out, she glanced at her watch. Ten minutes since the last one.

Don't panic, she told herself. *Don't panic.*

The door flew open. Ramos appeared.

'Are you ready to sign?' he asked.

She took a deep breath. 'Have you got the papers retracting your evidence?'

'It's in hand. As soon as our marriage licence is signed it will be lodged.'

Flora closed her eyes briefly then focused them on the document in her hand. Figures with lots of zeros flashed before her but she paid them scant attention. All she needed to check was that it dealt only with the financial side of their marriage and it did.

'Can I have a pen, please?' she asked the woman.

A pen was produced and a table pushed to her.

Marry Ramos and set her brother free.

Marry Ramos and tie herself to the most loathsome man on the planet.

Justin won.

Flora signed.

Ramos's smile was pure satisfaction. 'Time for us to marry.'

CHAPTER THREE

IGNORING RAMOS'S OUTSTRETCHED hand of help, Flora hoisted herself onto her feet.

Her baby was coming.

She'd get the farce of a wedding done with, ensure Ramos kept his word about Justin, and then she would tell him he was going to be a father imminently.

Plenty of time, she assured herself. Ten minutes between contractions was fine. Her English midwife had told her she probably wouldn't be admitted into hospital until the contractions were four minutes apart. That would likely take hours. Right now, she needed to concentrate on Justin's freedom. She had no idea how Ramos would react to her being in labour and didn't dare risk telling him just yet.

She was in labour!

A zing of pure excitement flooded her. Her baby was coming!

Soon, very, very soon, she would meet her baby.

'I assume the financial package is to your liking,' Ramos observed as they walked up the corridor.

The tone of his voice made her curious. 'Sorry?'

He shrugged. 'You were smiling.'

'Oh. Right. You assumed I was smiling about the money?'

'In a few minutes you are going to be a very wealthy woman.'

His cynical assumption barely doused the excitement still rippling inside her. *Her baby was coming!*

'Just set my brother free. That's all I care about.'

And that my baby is born safe and healthy.

'Sure.'

She stopped walking and faced him. 'Believe what you like, Ramos…' oh, she did enjoy the tightening on his face when she addressed him by his surname '…but I'm marrying you for Justin's freedom. You will never—'

Her intention of telling him he would never be a husband to her in the true sense of the word was cut from her tongue when another contraction hit.

Luckily she was close to a wall and slammed a hand on it to steady herself, and managed to focus on her watch. Uh oh. Nine minutes.

'Flora?'

For the first time she detected concern in Ramos's voice.

She waved her other hand at him and rode the wave of pain. 'Heartburn,' she managed to gasp.

As soon as she felt it start to abate, she breathed deeply and got walking again. 'Where are we marrying?'

'The civil court in the building next door.'

'Okay.'

Just breathe.

'Are you sure you're all right?'

'Yep. Let's get this done.' She upped her pace. She had eight or nine minutes until the next contraction hit.

As luck would have it, there was no need

for them to go outside as there was an internal passageway adjoining the two court buildings.

'I need to use the bathroom,' she said once they were in the civil courts, and headed for the door with the sign for the ladies on it.

She closed the door right at the moment the next contraction struck.

Once it had subsided, she splashed water on her face and looked in the mirror. Immediately, she wished she hadn't. Her shoulder-length chestnut hair, usually so glossy, was lank, her usually golden cheeks flush. Even her eyes—alien eyes, her brother always called them, on account of them being so large—had lost their sparkle.

And no wonder.

She was in labour and about to marry Ramos.

Flora had never imagined herself marrying. Men didn't hang around, something she'd known since she was small. Women were disposable. For Ramos, as with her father and her brother, this was especially true.

And if she had imagined it—and she'd be a liar if she didn't admit the odd idle daydream of a wedding day had sneaked up on her over the years—the faceless groom had been someone who worshipped her, who swore to never stray, who swore to love her as she got older and her looks faded. Someone she worshipped in return.

Not this: coerced into a shotgun marriage where the only emotion between the bride and groom was mutual loathing.

It wasn't loathing that had led to their child's conception...

She cut that thought straight off.

Ramos was waiting for her outside the bathroom door. He looked at her closely.

'Come on,' she insisted before he could say anything. Her brother's freedom was minutes away. 'Let's get married.'

The next contraction struck seconds after the 'ceremony' began. This time she was seated next to Ramos, the official on the other side of the desk busy directing all his conversation at him, so she was able to ride through it without either of them noticing.

All Flora was required to do was hand over her passport, give some details about herself and her parents and then it was time for her to repeat some words—the ceremony itself was conducted in English—just as Ramos had done, and sign the wedding certificate.

It was as she leaned forward to sign that a contraction hit her that was so strong she was helpless to stop the groan of pain from escaping.

'Flora?' This time there was alarm in Ramos's voice.

Not daring to look at him, she squeezed her eyes shut and gripped her fingertips onto the table. When it had passed, she grabbed the pen and signed.

Only then did she look at Ramos.

'We're done,' she said hoarsely. 'Now free my brother.'

Not taking his eyes from her face, he said something that sounded like an order to the official, then murmured to her, 'Let me get you some water.'

'Free my...*oh*.'

She focused on Ramos's face. Properly focused. Gazed into his worried eyes. And then she looked down at the puddle of water forming between her feet.

Another contraction hit and this time panic hit with it.

The time between contractions was coming too quickly and she couldn't stop the fear from showing when she met Ramos's appalled stare.

'It is coming now?' he asked faintly.

She nodded.

He sprang into action.

Jumping to his feet, he flung the door open and shouted out an order into the corridor while simultaneously putting his phone to his ear and barking an order at whoever answered it.

In what felt like hours but was in reality a couple of minutes at most, Ramos had an arm around her and was gently helping her into a wheelchair.

'An ambulance is on its way,' he said in a soothing tone she'd never heard him speak with before. 'You're going to Monte Cleure's best hospital. Its top obstetrician is on his way and will have everything ready for when you arrive.'

She focused on his eyes and nodded jerkily.

She could do this. She could do this. She was prepared. She could do this.

Soon she was being wheeled into the back of an ambulance breathing into a portable gas and air tank.

Ramos hung back to speak to a paramedic and then the panic really hit her.

Her baby was coming. Throughout the pregnancy her midwife had spoken about the importance of a birthing partner but Flora had shrugged off her concerns and brightly assured her—and assured herself—that she could do it alone.

The truth was, there had been no one to ask.

She loved her brother but the thought of him being in the birthing room was too icky to contemplate, even if she had thought he'd be free to be there. Also, Justin was spectacularly squeamish. Same with her deadbeat father, who'd probably turn up a week after she called him. Her extended family had turned against Justin and so turned against Flora for supporting him. Her old tight-knit group of school friends all had busy lives and now all lived too far away to reliably be there. She'd made a few new friends since her move to London but there was no real closeness, no one she could turn to.

So she'd prepared herself to go through the birth alone just as she'd had to swallow her fears and prepare herself for raising her child alone too. She'd truly thought she was mentally ready for it but, now that the moment was here, terror at what lay ahead struck and as soon as Ramos was back by her side she removed the tube from her mouth and grabbed his hand.

'Don't leave me,' she begged. 'Please, don't leave me.'

A furrow formed in his brow. 'You want me to come to the hospital?'

Another contraction gripped her and she shoved the tube into her mouth and breathed in and out with it, squeezing Ramos's hand so tightly in the process he winced at the strength of it.

'Please,' she panted when the worst of it was over, uncaring that tears were rolling down her face. 'I don't want to do this alone.

Please, Alejandro, don't make me do this alone. Please.'

He studied her intently a moment longer before his features softened. Smoothing her hair off her forehead with the hand not being squeezed to death, he placed a kiss to it. 'I won't leave your side. I promise.'

And just like that, the fear that had snuck up on her and come close to smothering her lessened and she flopped her head back.

'Thank you,' she breathed with relief.

'Shoot me,' Flora begged Ramos in the birthing room when the latest contraction subsided enough for her to speak. 'Please. Get a gun and shoot me.'

The midwife smiled sympathetically. She'd heard it all before.

Ramos kissed the fingers gripping his hand so tightly. His other hand was rubbing her lower back. 'I know it hurts, *querida*. You hold onto me, okay? You can do this.'

'I *can't.*'

He kissed her fingers again. 'You can. I have every faith in you. You're beautiful and brave and strong, just hold on a little longer. You're almost there.'

Two hours later, Ramos gently placed their son back to her breast and pulled the visitor's chair as close to her bed in the private room she'd been moved to as he could get. His eyes were shining with wonder and pride. 'He's perfect.'

High on the precious little bundle whose precious little face was nuzzling into her skin and high on the release of hormones flooding her system, Flora felt her chest swell with so much love she thought it might burst out of her.

She gazed at Ramos and took in his stubbly jaw, creased shirt and dishevelled hair. She'd never seen him anything but immaculately groomed before and the sight of him like this and the knowledge of *why* he was like this filled her chest even more.

He was all dishevelled because he'd spent six hours right by her side, four of those being used as her human form of pain relief.

The pain was already a distant memory.

'He looks like you,' she said dreamily.

He traced his fingers lightly over their son's head. 'Do you think?'

She nodded and smothered a yawn. 'Just like you.'

His broad shoulders rose and he gazed into her eyes with the same sense of wonder he kept staring at their son with. 'I'm so proud of you.'

Feeling a blush form on her cheeks, she tried to make light of it. 'Aw, shucks, it was nothing.'

He snickered but then the amusement faded and the wonder in his stare returned. 'Thank you for letting me share that.'

'Thank you for being there.' He'd been wonderful. It was an unselfish, giving, empathetic side to him that she'd forgotten existed, but she had seen that side of him before, in the months leading to her mother's death. Ramos's regular visits had never failed to bring a smile to her mum's face.

'Sorry about your fingers,' she added sleepily.

The grin returned. 'My own birthing war wound.'

Another yawn crept up on her before she

could cover it, a wave of exhaustion hitting her like a sledgehammer.

Ramos noticed. Lifting their son from her arms, he gently said, 'Sleep, *querida*. I will wake you when he's ready for another feed.'

Her 'thank you' had barely left her lips before sleep claimed her.

'Have you chosen a name for him yet?' Ramos asked soon after his return from a quick shopping trip for baby clothes and provisions. He'd bought so many cute little outfits that there was no way their baby would wear them all before he outgrew them.

Night had long fallen. Their little boy had just been fed and was now sleeping in his daddy's arms dressed in an adorable romper suit.

Happily exhausted, Flora nestled her cheek deeper into her pillow and gazed at her husband and son.

Her husband and son...

This was going to take a lot of getting her head around.

'I always thought if it was a boy I would

call him Benjamin for my grandfather. Do you have any ideas?'

'You did all the hard work. You should choose. If you want to call him Benjamin then I have no objections.'

'You're his father. You should have a say.' And the way he'd been during the birth and the way he was behaving towards them now showed he wanted to *be* a father. This was something she hadn't dared hope for her child, not after the way Ramos had severed her from his life, but, having grown up with her father on the periphery of her life, Flora would always choose for her child to have more if it was possible. She'd forgotten that the man who could be so vengefully cruel when crossed had a generous heart when touched, and it made her chest swell to see that heart so touched by his own flesh and blood.

For a long moment he just stared at her before a wry smile spread on his face. 'I am struggling to get my head around being a father. This whole day has been...' He shook his head, clearly unable to find the right words.

'A roller coaster?' she suggested. That's exactly how it felt for her. At least she'd had a good seven months to prepare for motherhood. Ramos had had little more than seven hours to prepare for fatherhood. Yes, it was his own fault but, in her softened, hormonal baby state, Flora could appreciate how overwhelming it must be for him.

'*Sí*. A roller coaster,' he agreed. 'This is not at all how I expected my day to end.'

'I didn't expect my day to end like this either. I thought I had three weeks left before this little one came along, and I definitely didn't think I would end it as the wife of my mortal enemy.'

The wry smile turned into a grin that in itself evolved into a snicker. 'A rather extreme method of calling a truce.'

'Who said anything about a truce?' she said lightly. 'This is a mere suspension of hostilities.'

'A ceasefire?'

'Exactly. And it's a ceasefire I think we should do our best to hold, for this little one's sake.'

'I'm glad you think that. I don't want there to be war between us, *querida*.'

Understanding flowed between them that, for their son, they were both prepared to make the best of things.

Flora dragged her stare from him and settled it on their son in his arms.

She sighed.

She had to be careful and remember who she'd married.

Sharing the birth had bonded them—how could it not have?—but she mustn't let the hormones and euphoria flooding her cloud her judgement or soften her too much against him. Whenever there was a high, a low was sure to follow. These magical first hours with their baby wouldn't last. Ramos was still Ramos.

But, for now, it was the three of them cocooned together and she was glad her little boy got to bond with his father.

'Are there any names that are special or meaningful to you?' she asked. 'What about your father's name? Rafael, isn't it?'

He pulled a dismissive face. 'No.'

That surprised her. She knew little about

Ramos's father other than that he was supremely wealthy and went through wives as if they were going out of fashion, but she'd always had the impression father and son were close. 'Why not?'

'Just, no.'

'Oi.' She stretched an arm out and jabbed a finger to his arm. 'We've only been married a few hours. You can't start keeping secrets from me yet, you know.'

Melting dark eyes held hers before crinkling and looking down at their son nestled so securely in his strong arms. 'My father is selfish. He's always been selfish.'

She gave a sympathetic smile. 'We finally have something in common.'

His gaze fell back on her. 'Yes. We both have selfish fathers.'

There was little of Flora's life Ramos didn't already know. He'd been an intrinsic part of it for many years.

'What was your mother like?' she asked. For obvious reasons—the obvious being that she'd spent more than half her life actively avoiding conversation with him—she knew little about his childhood and home life apart from the things Justin had mentioned. She knew his mother had died of sepsis when he was ten, the only story Justin had ever related to her about Ramos that had made her heart pang for him.

'Bossy.' His mouth made a swirling motion. 'Very bossy. And very good at getting her own way. Like a sensei. She would make me put my toys away or straighten my clothes just by looking at me.'

She smiled. 'My mum could be like that too. With Justin. Not me. I always put my toys away.' Flora's mum had more than made up for her useless father.

'I remember,' he said drily. 'You were always such a serious child.'

'Not always.'

'Always when I saw you. And disapproving of me too—I would walk into a room and your little nose would go in the air.'

He was more perceptive than she'd credited. Ramos was so staggeringly arrogant she'd assumed he'd never noticed her hostility.

'I thought you were a bad influence on Justin,' she admitted.

A shadow immediately fell on his face. 'No one can be a bad influence on him,' he denied tautly.

'You were.'

'No.'

'He was always trying to impress you.'

He shrugged. 'Most people try to impress me.' The shadow lifted and a smile played on his lips. 'You are one of the rare exceptions.'

Unsure whether he was complimenting her or not, unsure whether she wanted it to be a compliment or not, she cautiously asked, 'Where is he?'

'Hillier? Probably celebrating his reprieve in a hotel bar with a woman or two on his arm.'

She ignored the slight on her brother's morals. They were traits he'd picked up from this man, but, with her body and emotions softened from her newborn baby, not something she wanted to think about right then.

'So he is free?'

'That was the deal.' An edge had come into his voice. 'Hillier gets away with stealing from me and can resume his life as if nothing happened.'

'Hardly. His life is ruined.'

His eyes turned cold. 'He has no one to blame but himself.'

'He knows that.' She swallowed. 'He's desperate to make amends with you.'

'He could start by repaying the million euros he stole from me but seeing as he stole from my casino to repay debts incurred at my rival's casino, I will never see that money again.'

'He was in over his head and not in his right mind,' she reminded him quietly. 'You know how badly Mum's death affected him.'

He knew too how close and protective her brother had been of his mother and sister, the self-proclaimed man of the house since the age of seven when their mum had kicked their dad out. All those weekends Ramos spent in the Hillier family home were because his party animal best mate needed to satisfy himself the females in his family were well.

Justin might have hidden the depths of his despair at her death from Ramos, but Ramos knew all about it because Flora had explained most of it to him the night she'd turned up at his home.

He'd heard her out. His expression had been inscrutable as she'd explained how Justin had developed a gambling addiction and how the owners of the casino he'd been secretly going to had continually extended his credit until he owed them a few grand shy of a million euros. The dark swirling in Ramos's eyes had convinced her she was getting through to him, but she'd never had the chance to lay everything out because the dark swirling had intensified and...

And she didn't want to remember what happened next. It had been madness. Heavenly madness.

Jaw clenched, Ramos tilted his head back and fixed his gaze on the ceiling. When he eventually spoke it was through teeth that were clearly gritted together. 'My mother died when I was a child. I didn't use that as an excuse to lie and cheat and steal, and I cannot believe that your mother would accept her death as an excuse for Hillier to do all that to me.'

'Mum would be devastated about it,' Flora

agreed. 'He's behaved terribly but he wasn't in his right mind, I swear, and if you would agree to see him and let him—'

'I will never see him again,' he cut in, dropping his gaze back on her with a stare that brooked no argument. 'And Benjamin is to have nothing to do with him either, is that understood?'

'He's my brother,' she reminded him lowly.

His nostrils flared. 'I'm not going to stop you from seeing him but he's a liar and a thief and I don't want Benjamin anywhere near him.'

For a moment, Flora eyeballed him back, but only for a moment.

This was the most momentous day of her life and she didn't want to ruin the magic of her son's birth for a battle she was unlikely to win. Not yet, anyway. Maybe one day.

There was a tightening in her chest to realise she'd committed herself to many days as his wife. Thousands of them. For her beautiful, precious boy's sake, she would do her best to spend them in peace.

'Benjamin?' she whispered softly.

Ramos's dark eyes narrowed in suspicion

before the glare on his face melted away and he bestowed her with a smile that made her heart expand. '*Sí*. Benjamin. It's a good name. I like it.'

She couldn't believe how much this pleased her. 'Then you should choose his middle name.'

'There is one obvious choice for that.'

'Which is...?'

'Alejandro,' he answered smugly.

CHAPTER FOUR

THE NEXT FEW days spent recovering in hospital passed in a blurry whirl. Ramos didn't leave their side, going as far as to cram his tall frame into a single foldable bed provided by the hospital every night. Anything Flora wanted, he made sure she got, whether it was a cup of tea or a bowl of her favourite comfort food: macaroni cheese. He gave her an arm to lean on when she needed to walk across the room to the bathroom or wanted to sit outside with their son in the shaded pretty hospital garden. She drew the line at him helping her to bath, however, and got the ever-helpful nurse assigned to her to assist instead. Birth had stripped her of any dignity she had, but that had been an exceptional circumstance and one she had no intention of dwelling on.

The little bubble the three of them formed was never destined to last though, and on the third morning Flora was filled with sadness when she and Benjamin were discharged. She was also filled with resolve.

She and Ramos had proved they could get on. They'd proved they could be effective parents together. She would start her married life with a positive frame of mind and hope that they could make their marriage work as best it could under the circumstances of its founding. She had no illusions about the man she'd married but would take it one day at a time.

Ramos had had her dress dry-cleaned. He'd also conjured up a hairbrush for her, which was just as well as the second they stepped out of the hospital's main door they were greeted with the blinding flash of cameras and questions being lobbed from every direction.

Instinctively, she clung to Ramos's arm and pressed herself close to his side. He carried Benjamin in the car seat he'd had delivered to the hospital earlier that morning, and wrapped his free arm protectively around her.

Barely seconds could have passed before

the jostling crowd was pushed back by four no-nonsense man mountains, but they didn't move back far enough for Flora not to hear their shouts. Most of them were in French and Spanish but she caught a few English ones too.

'Is the baby yours, Alejandro?'

'Are you going to have a DNA test?'

'Was this a trap to get him to drop the charges against your brother, Flora?'

'How long have you two been lovers?'

'What do you think of the footage of Aimee crying, Alejandro?'

'Did you forget to tell Aimee you were having an affair, Alejandro?'

And then she was being ushered into the back of a huge black four-by-four with darkened windows, the doors closed and the only sound her son's cries.

Flora soothed Benjamin as best she could while Ramos secured the car seat between them. When he was done and Benjamin was strapped in the seat, he tapped on the screen dividing them from the driver and bodyguard up front.

The car slowly crawled away.

Benjamin's cries soon quietened. Only when she was certain that he was asleep did Flora turn her stare to Ramos.

'Who's Aimee?'

The silence before he answered went on so long she could have boiled a kettle and made herself a pot of tea.

If he had answered immediately with, 'My girlfriend, but it's over, I'm married to you now,' Flora would have been fine. Or so she liked to think.

The reality was very different.

'Aimee was my mistress.'

Revulsion was instantaneous. 'Pardon me? Your *mistress*?'

He inclined his head.

'What do you mean by mistress? Isn't a mistress a married man's lover?'

'Not always.'

Her heart pounding, she waited for him to elaborate.

'Well?' she said when the silence grew.

'Well, what?'

'Are you going to explain it to me?'

'For what purpose?'

'Oh, let me think… Because I'm your wife and I deserve to know?'

'Or so you can judge me?' he challenged, finally turning his stare on her.

'I wouldn't.'

His top lip curled. 'You're judging me now. I can tell. You have always judged me.'

She clamped her lips together, unable to deny this latest evidence of his astuteness.

What she didn't dare tell him was that she'd never really judged him from a moral perspective, but more from an instinctive revulsion that she had only ever experienced for him and never her brother, who'd got through women with the same reckless speed.

His eyes narrowed and firm lips tightened at her silence. 'You used to give the impression you didn't think me worthy to breathe the same air as you. The first time you looked at me as if I wasn't something your cat had brought in was when you came to me to plead for your brother. That was the first time *you* instigated a conversation. I made every effort with you but you always made it clear you didn't care for my efforts.

I wasn't good enough for you to look in the eye or talk to until you wanted something from me.'

Her stomach twisted.

Desperation to free her brother from a foreign prison had driven Flora to Ramos. Desperate times called for desperate measures and if she'd had to get down on her knees and beg him to drop the charges against Justin and come up with a way of punishing him that wouldn't have him sentenced to twenty years of imprisonment, then she would have done it.

Even so, she'd had to summon all the courage she possessed to announce herself at his gate. Five minutes it had taken for permission to be granted, and she'd felt every second of it. Then she'd had to find the courage to knock on his door. When he'd opened it, she'd pulled out one last scrap of courage to look into the eyes of the man whose gaze she'd spent years avoiding.

He'd stared at her without speaking for the longest time.

She'd been unable to speak too. Her tongue

had become tied. Everything she'd planned to say had spirited out of her brain.

And then he'd blinked, run his fingers through his hair, and invited her inside.

He'd been barefoot, she remembered with a pang.

It made her skin burn to remember how she'd walked out of the same door the next morning feeling as if she were floating on a cloud only to end the day in despair.

The promise to meet in the lobby of the hotel she was staying in had never materialised. She'd made two calls that evening, one to his mobile, which hadn't connected, the other to his house. The person on the other end had curtly informed her Señor Ramos was unavailable and that she mustn't call again.

Nausea swirled in the pit of her stomach to know why he'd stood her up and cut her from his life. To know he still believed that of her.

Forcing herself to maintain eye contact, she whispered, 'What happened between us... I didn't sleep with you for Justin's sake, I swear.'

Ramos's jaw clenched. There was a long pause before he challenged, 'Then why did you?'

'You were there.' She swallowed. 'You know why.'

It was because she couldn't not.

At the time she'd thought it was because he couldn't not too.

His chest rose sharply. She could feel him trying to probe into her brain. She wished she could delve into his mind too, and scoop out his memories of their night together and see if it had meant anything to him. Anything at all.

Frightened at how badly she wished it *had* meant something to him, Flora cleared her throat and strove for lightness, desperate to break the charged silence. 'So... Was Aimee your lover...when we...' she couldn't bring herself to call it making love even though that was how it had felt at the time '...slept together?'

Eyes not leaving her face, he rested his head back. 'She was my mistress, not my lover,' he corrected. 'A mistress is a woman kept by a man. I paid for her apartment and gave her an allowance and in return...' He raised a shoulder.

'And in return she kept herself available for you?' Flora guessed hoarsely. Her stomach rippled violently in the same way it had when she'd seen those paparazzi pictures of him and Justin sailing the Mediterranean on Ramos's yacht with a dozen topless, beautiful women sunbathing around them.

He gave a slow incline of his head.

'Were you faithful to her?'

'There is no exclusivity between a man and his mistress. That is the whole point.'

'Then why has she been crying?' And why did *she* feel like crying?

'Because she's an actress—a professional one—seeking attention. Playing the wronged lover is a role she can get her teeth into.'

'Or, maybe, she's genuinely upset.'

'Very conveniently when the paparazzi are there to witness it,' he rebutted drily. 'We have been over for a long time.'

Noting that he'd avoided answering if Aimee had still been his mistress when they'd slept together, and on the verge of asking if he still intended to take lovers now they were married, she was cut off by the sound of his phone ringing before she could voice it.

Grateful for the interruption, Flora turned her face away to gaze out of the window and breathed in deeply.

Of course he would have lovers. Alejandro Ramos was a Lothario with the looks and wealth to live exactly as he pleased with no need for thought or consideration for anyone else. Any woman who kidded herself into believing otherwise was on a hiding to nothing but heartbreak. She'd been stupid enough to fool herself once that she might be different from the others, and he'd mentally cut her from his life before she'd got out of his bed. She would not put herself in the position of making that mistake again.

She was going to have to keep her heart sealed in titanium because this was a marriage she wouldn't be able to escape for many years. He'd already warned her of the consequences should she divorce him but, now that Benjamin was here, she was prepared to give their marriage a proper chance for their son's sake, because Ramos was his father and, most importantly, *wanted* to be a father to him.

She really hoped that Aimee woman's tears were fake. As repulsive as she found the whole mistress thing, she wouldn't wish harm or pain on anyone.

They'd reached the Spanish border.

She wished they could be back in the private hospital room, the three of them cocooned without any intrusion from the outside world.

The rest of the two-hour drive to Ramos's villa in the Pedralbes area of Barcelona was spent in silence broken only by the low murmur of his voice as he made numerous calls. Benjamin slept the entire journey. Still exhausted from the birth, Flora slept much of it too.

She didn't expect her heart to thud when they drove through the electric gates to his land. She'd only been here twice before. Both times it had been dark, the three-storey villa designed in the style of a French mansion aglow with soft, romantic nightlights. The last time, she'd parked her hire car against the high privacy wall and climbed marble steps, freshly awed at the ornately created wrought iron balconies each front-facing window was adorned with.

This time it was daylight, the sun high above them and casting the white exterior with a warm glow. This time, she was driven into a brightly lit underground garage in which seven other vehicles, including a motorbike, were already parked.

As if he had an internal radar, Benjamin's eyes opened. And then his mouth opened and the silence officially ended. Flora unclipped him, lifted him into her arms and carried him out of the car.

'I will show you to your room,' Ramos said as they stepped into an elevator.

Her room?

He must have registered the shock in her eyes for he smiled faintly. 'I thought you would prefer your own space while you settle in and recover. You will be in the guest room next to mine so I will be close by if you need me.'

Her stomach plunged but whether in relief or disappointment she couldn't tell.

With everything that had happened these

last few days, the sleeping arrangements here were not something she'd allowed herself to think about but on some subconscious level she must have assumed she would share Ramos's room, because wasn't that what married people did?

The elevator door opened into the same reception room she'd first stepped into three years ago for his twenty-eighth birthday party. Directly ahead, through a wide, open archway, was the main vast living area with a ceiling so high she'd had to crane her neck fully back to see it. Her entire childhood home, floor to roof, could fit in a third of that one space. The other side of the living space led to the outdoor entertaining area where the party had been held.

With an unsettled Benjamin in her arms, they headed straight up the wide winding stairs to the first floor. Flora followed Ramos along the open galleried section of the landing that overlooked the main living area and held her breath as they neared the bedroom where she'd so willingly, foolishly, given herself to him.

If she hadn't seen Ramos's bedroom, she would have gasped at the splendour she'd been appointed. Her room—or suite, as it should really be called, but even that was to do it a disservice—was breathtaking. A princess of royal birth would be delighted to call this her own, and if she weren't feeling so low and if Benjamin's cries weren't becoming more vocal by the second, she would be bruising herself with pinches to believe this was to be hers.

A crib had been placed next to the emperor bed that in itself was approximately half the size of Ramos's own bed.

'I assumed you would want him to sleep with you while you are still feeding him,' he said.

Flora nodded. Benjamin needed feeding right now. She'd had no problem feeding him with Ramos around in the hospital but it felt different here in the intimacy of a bedroom, and as she realised this she realised he must have anticipated she would feel like this and that was why he'd given her her own private space.

He must have sensed her awkwardness for

he bowed his head. 'I will leave you to it. I will show you the nursery and everything else when you are ready. Shall I get Madeline to bring you tea?'

'Who's Madeline?'

'My housekeeper.'

'Yes, please.' But as she spoke a tear rolled down her cheek. She had no idea where it came from or why it was followed by another, and another, but before she knew it her cheeks were sodden.

'Hey.' Ramos crouched in front of her.

She managed to wipe her eyes clear.

He brushed a strand of hair off her face. 'What is the matter?'

She sniffed but it did nothing to stop more tears from falling. 'I don't know.'

And she didn't. Flora didn't have a clue what she was crying about.

'You don't like your room?'

She managed a laugh. 'It's beautiful. I think maybe this is what they call The Baby Blues.'

Sympathetic understanding lit his face and he brushed another lock of her hair. 'You concentrate on taking care of Benjamin. Let me take care of you and everything else. Okay?'

She bit into her wobbling bottom lip as she breathed in deeply and nodded.

The whisper of a smile quirked on his cheeks before he gently kissed her forehead. 'I will get the tea organised for you.'

And then he was gone, leaving Flora touching the scorching mark on her forehead made by his lips.

There was a tap on her bedroom door.

Flora, her stomach churning, braced herself before calling, 'Come in.'

Ramos appeared, suited and booted and looking all hunky and fresh. 'I'm going now.'

'Safe travels,' she said brightly, determined he should think she wasn't in the slightest bit bothered about him leaving.

Ramos owned an international chain of mammoth hotel casino complexes. He'd taken three weeks off work to be there for her and Benjamin, and now it was time for him to return to the working world. He was easing himself in gently. Today was the start of only five nights away in Rome.

Only.

He lifted Benjamin from her arms and said, 'The press have gone.'

He smelt as fresh and spicy as he looked and her despondency grew. She was still in her pyjamas. She hadn't even run a brush through her hair. She must look a right state.

And Ramos, who she knew for a fact hadn't had sex in at least three weeks on account of him not leaving the villa, was heading to a city filled with some of the world's most beautiful, sophisticated women.

She must not think like this. Ramos could do what he liked.

'Good,' she answered. And it was good. The press had been camped outside the villa's grounds since she'd arrived. She guessed they'd finally moved on to a fresher story.

'There are bodyguards to escort you when you're ready to go out,' he told her. 'Let Madeline know and she will make the arrangements. If you need anything at all, speak to her.'

'Okay.' She kept the nonchalance in her tone by the skin of her teeth. Her heart was feeling bluer by the passing second.

He kissed Benjamin's cheek then carefully passed him back to her, dark eyes scrutinising.

For one silly moment Flora held her breath in anticipation that he would kiss her cheek too. Other than the brushing of arms when lifting Benjamin between them, he hadn't touched her since that comforting kiss on her forehead when she first moved in.

He took a step back. 'If you want me to stay, I can rearrange things.'

Lightly stroking Benjamin's back, she injected even more brightness into her voice. 'Don't be silly. We'll be fine.'

'You are sure?'

'Haven't I already told you that a thousand times? Go on, shoo. Rome is waiting with bated breath for you.'

She managed to wait until he'd closed the door behind him before bursting into tears.

Benjamin was sound asleep.

Flora wished she could drift off too but her head, so hot and heavy from newborn baby sleep deprivation, was too full of Ramos to sleep. She couldn't stop herself from wonder-

ing where he was and what he was doing...
And who he was doing it with.

He was on his third business trip in two
weeks. This time he'd gone to London, just
mentioned casually the day before he left that
he'd be visiting his Mayfair casino for three
days. She'd held her breath waiting for him
to invite her and Benjamin with him to her
home city, but nothing.

She supposed a wife and newborn baby
would cramp his style.

Those early days and weeks when they'd
found a harmony together were nothing but a
distant memory. She often wondered if she'd
dreamt them because, since he'd returned to
work, in the much reduced time they spent
together conversation had become stiltedly
polite and only ever concerned their son.

Wiping away more tears that had sprung
from nowhere—she wished she didn't cry all
the time but could do nothing to stop them—
she gave herself a good talking to.

Flora had married Ramos for her brother's
freedom. Ramos had married her for their
son. That was all there was between them
and she had better get used to it. When he

was home he was a good, hands-on father. She must stop torturing herself about the women he shared his nights with. No good could come from it. All it would do would make her bitter and she had no right to be bitter, not when she was raising her son in a luxury she could never have dreamed of for him.

If Ramos had presented this marriage to her from the outset; a marriage where they had separate rooms, where he worked away for the majority of his time and where relations between them were cordially polite when home, she might not have needed to be blackmailed into agreeing to it.

These baby blue hormones would pass soon, she assured herself, and, when they did, all her emotions would return to an even keel and Ramos would mean nothing more to her than the man she shared a child and a roof with.

CHAPTER FIVE

FIVE MONTHS AFTER giving birth and moving to Barcelona, Flora finally felt like her old self. She'd come out of the baby fugue. She hadn't cried in at least a month. It helped that Benjamin now slept through the night, meaning she slept soundly through the night too.

With sleep deprivation a thing of the past, she began to see and feel things more clearly. Her love for her son had formed when the pregnancy stick had shown the positive sign and swelled from there. In the fugue after the birth she'd carried that swell of love every second of the day but now it had become more defined, encapsulated within the certainty that she would sooner throw herself in front of a speeding train than let harm come to a single hair on his precious head.

Unfortunately, her awareness for Ramos had become more defined too.

The days he was home, all the tiny atoms

that made her became fully charged, creating a buzz in her skin and a burr in her brain. Her heart would thump painfully. The very air she breathed tasted different.

If her presence had any effect on him, he hid it well, but why should she affect him when he had any number of women to keep him entertained when he was away on business, women who didn't bear the scars of a belly that had so recently been swollen to the size of a watermelon? And he was away on business far more than he was home. It was probably why he'd not bothered moving her into his room or made any intimations to make their marriage anything more than two people who shared a child and a roof.

She never asked him about the women. It was none of her business, she reminded herself staunchly and often. It was obvious their marriage was in name only and, with all the stupid effects he had on her, that was just as well.

Not that the opportunity to ask about his women ever arose. Not any more. In the month since she'd stopped feeding Benjamin herself and moved him into his nursery, communication between them had deteriorated further. Now, when Ramos was home, she passed their son into his willing, capable hands, filled him in on anything new or that he'd missed, and then made her escape, usually to her suite, until it was time to hand over again.

It was safer keeping her distance from him, but the distance was not having the effect she so needed it to have. Right now he was over halfway through a two week visit to his majestic hotel casino in Las Vegas, his only non-European enterprise. He'd never been away so far or for so long before and, far from her rejoicing at this extra distance, her stomach had been tied in knots for every minute he'd been gone.

All she wanted was to find an emotional neutrality with him to get her through their marriage until Benjamin was old enough to flee the nest. She would flee straight after. Ramos would have no reason to keep her.

But that was years and years away. The child who would one day grow into a man was currently a five-month-old baby who loved swimming, and it was for this love that Flora smothered Benjamin in sunscreen, and then put him in a swimming nappy and a one-piece swimsuit that gave extra protection to his delicate skin from the sun's rays.

Hoicking her swim-bag over her shoulder, she carried him downstairs, through the main living area and out of one of the three sets of French doors that led into the rear garden where her favourite of the three swimming pools was located. Well, her favourite to take Benjamin swimming in. She didn't particularly like the memories she had of it, but it had a lovely sized shallow end.

Leaving their towels on the sandstone tiles that surrounded the pool and the sprawling terrace area, she carried Benjamin into the shallow water and put him in an inflatable ring.

'Coming for a play?' she cheerfully asked Mateo, the young pool attendant. Of all the staff, Mateo was her favourite.

He looked over his shoulder and shook his head.

'Did you get into trouble with Madeline the other day?' He'd joined them in the pool for ten minutes and had made Benjamin squeal his head off with glee.

He pulled a face and looked at the ground.

The housekeeper ran a very tight ship with the staff. Unobtrusive decorum was expected at all times. It was a mystery to Flora why Mateo had been employed. She'd never known an unobtrusive, decorous eighteen-year-old in her life. She imagined he'd taken the job expecting to be pool and bar attendant to wild parties with *muchos* semi-naked ladies like the one Flora had briefly attended, not for the only excitement in his working week to come from the new *señora*'s daily swim with the baby.

He would have been in heaven if he'd worked here when Ramos held his twenty-eighth birthday party.

'Madeline cannot tell you off if *I* give the order, okay?' she said, speaking slowly.

The look he gave her told her Madeline could and probably would.

Flora smothered a sigh.

When she'd moved in, she'd been physically and emotionally fragile from the birth, and so been glad of Madeline's cool authority. She'd become gradually less glad of it because it had become patently clear that the housekeeper had *all* the authority. The *señora* of the house—Flora refused to refer to herself as the mistress—had none.

Since the baby fog had lifted, Flora had become certain Madeline reported on her to Ramos. She hoped it was just paranoia on her own part.

'Okay, no getting in the pool, then. Can we practise my Spanish?'

That was something no one could scold Mateo for. No one else had time to teach her.

'Castellano,' he corrected, sitting down on the pool's edge. He dragged his fingers into the water and flicked it at Benjamin, who giggled.

'Castellano,' she repeated. She'd considered learning Catalan rather than Spanish—Castellano—but then realised Ramos was conversing with Benjamin in the latter. She didn't want it to get to the stage where her son and husband talked between themselves and she couldn't understand any of it.

She pushed Benjamin's inflatable ring back and forth while Mateo continued to flick water at him, laughing and repeating words in Spanish over her son's delighted squeals.

'You all look as if you're having fun.'

Flora didn't think she'd ever seen someone get to their feet as quickly as Mateo did at Ramos's deep rumble. And she didn't think her heart had ever thrown itself as hard against her ribcage as it did then either.

She lifted Benjamin into her arms, then, pulses racing, turned around to face her husband.

Painfully aware that even using Benjamin as a shield didn't hide the lumps and bumps on her body that her plain black swimsuit couldn't disguise, Flora managed to find a pleasant smile to greet him with and speak over the staccato of her heart. 'You're back early. I wasn't expecting you until the weekend.'

'Obviously.' He fixed his laser stare on an obviously frightened Mateo and barked an order at him.

The young lad scuttled off.

The laser stare zoomed back on her. 'We will talk about this when Benjamin is sleeping.'

'Talk about what?' she asked, confused at the dark fury on his face and confused about why it was directed at her.

His face contorted. He held up his forefinger as if to gesticulate before shaking his head. 'I will not be made a fool of in my own home, Flora.'

And then he stalked away, leaving Flora staring at his retreating figure in shock.

How was she supposed to have made a fool of him? If anyone had been made a fool of it was her. There was no way Ramos would return four days early from a work trip and not inform the household. No one, including him, had seen fit to tell her, his so-called wife.

Once they were both dry, she took Benjamin to the kitchen for some lunch. She'd recently started weaning him, something he'd taken well to, but today he kept his mouth tightly closed and shook his head so wildly she couldn't get the spoon near his mouth, never mind in it.

Flora understood his fractiousness. She felt it herself, her own fractiousness rising when she heard footsteps approach.

'Shall I try?'

She took a deep breath before jutting her chin and acknowledging Ramos's presence.

He'd changed out of his business suit, now wearing a pair of tan canvas shorts and a short-sleeved black shirt opened at the neck. He looked and smelled as fresh and gorgeous as if he were about to step into a photoshoot for a magazine specially featuring hunky, virile men, and her senses were totally overwhelmed with the potency of the whole Ramos package.

It only made her more conscious of her changed figure, and she thought miserably of the Vegas showgirls and other beautiful women he'd have just been surrounded by.

She wished she'd brought some clothes down with her and used the outside changing rooms to change into them. She wouldn't feel at such a disadvantage now, with only a beach towel hiding her ugliness.

Ramos's features were more relaxed than they'd been by the pool but his stare was still dark with anger when he trained it on her. It softened when he turned to their son.

Perching himself onto a stool next to Benjamin's high chair by the huge kitchen island, he chucked their son under the chin and spoke to him in Spanish before reaching for the plastic bowl with the mashed banana in it.

Benjamin opened his mouth and let the spoon go in.

Flora didn't know whether to laugh or cry.

Ramos lifted his gaze to her and dismissively said, 'I will finish feeding him. Go and put some clothes on.'

As Benjamin's back was to her she had no compunction in hitting Ramos with her most lethal stare, then sucked it away to kiss her son's cheek before finding even more venom to throw at the man who called himself her husband.

Fury propelled her up the stairs and to the sanctuary of her room.

How the hell did Ramos have the nerve to talk to her like that? To treat her like that?

He thought he wanted to talk to *her*? Oh,

he'd better wait. It was nothing on what she wanted to say to *him*.

Wriggling her way out of her swimsuit, she stomped past the rolltop bath and into her shower room without looking at her naked reflection. She hated looking at herself nude. Hated it.

When she'd been pregnant, she'd loved the changes pregnancy had made to her body. Even when she'd been at her biggest with permanently swollen feet and ankles she'd seen it as a rite of passage, leading to the day she met her child.

Now, whenever she caught sight of her post-pregnancy body, her stupid brain conjured up the women she'd seen pictured on Ramos's arm over the years, a parade of beauties with perfect complexions and perfect curves. Imagined Miranda, the impossibly beautiful woman who'd hung on his every word over that excruciating—for Flora—breakfast eleven years ago.

She wished she didn't care that he'd seen her nearly naked. Wished she didn't care how repelled he must have been to see the changes pregnancy had wrought.

'And she wished she knew what had made him so angry.

She didn't have to wait long to find out.

She was in her dressing room wearing only her knickers and bra, dithering over which dress to wear, when her bedroom door opened.

Her room was similar in design to Ramos's. Off the main sleeping area were two archways set at a right angle. One was the gateway to her bathrooms, the other to her dressing room. Heavy drapes could be closed to give privacy if wanted. Flora had never needed to close the drapes because Ramos rarely came in her room and when he did, he always knocked first and waited permission.

Whipping around, she saw the tall figure emerge. She yanked the closest item to hand off the rail to cover herself with, and scurried to the wall hidden from his view.

'Get out!' she half squealed, half shouted.

A deep, disembodied voice called back in a grim tone. 'After we have talked.'

Heart pounding hard, she pulled the item, a summery cream strapless dress, over her head. It was a dress she'd bought with a plan to shrink into it. She hadn't shrunk enough and, despite its supposedly forgiving elasticated, floaty design, looked and felt far too snug around her waist and hips. The bra she was wearing also looked ridiculous with it but no way was she taking that off.

The wall she was hiding behind had shelves of shorts and rails of T-shirts and tops she'd also bought with vague plans of shrinking into them. She found a pair of high-waisted denim shorts that landed mid-thigh and pulled them on under the dress. At least they did up without her having to breathe in too much, so that was a nice surprise. Flora then grabbed a loose lime-green kaftan and shoved it over her head. Only then did she pull the dress down to her feet and step out of it, and only then did she turn around and notice Ramos's reflection in the walled mirror on the far side. He was sitting on one of the plush rounded armchairs in her sleeping area.

He'd watched the entire charade.

With nowhere to hide, cheeks blazing with humiliation, she had no choice but to front it out.

Throwing herself into the armchair set at

an angle next to his, she glared at him. 'Have you never heard of knocking?'

'I have indeed.' His features were poker straight. Not even his eyes were giving anything away.

Flora wished she could be as controlled. 'Then why didn't you?'

'A man doesn't need permission to enter a room in his own home.'

'This might be your house but this is my room and you coming in without my permission is a gross invasion of my privacy.'

'Go and complain to someone who cares. Have you allowed your puppy dog in here?'

'What puppy dog?'

'*Your* puppy dog. Mateo. I understand you two have developed a certain…closeness.'

Understanding hit her. Flora's mouth opened but the understanding was so abhorrent that it took a few beats for anything to come out. 'You cannot be serious? I mean, seriously? You think I'm having an affair with Mateo?' Shaking her head, she laughed, not with humour but sheer disbelief.

'Are you?' An edge came into the tight control of his voice.

'Your mind belongs in the gutter.'

'Flora, I have asked you a question. Answer it.'

'Of course I'm not having an affair! He's a friend. Or am I not allowed friends?'

'He's an employee.'

'So what?'

'He was flirting with you.'

'Don't be ridiculous,' she snapped. 'He's nearly seven years younger than me.'

'And you are seven years younger than me. What's the difference?'

'I've just had a baby, that's the difference.'

'I saw you with my own eyes. Laughing together...'

'Oh, we were laughing, were we? Must be having an affair, then. No other reason for it. Well done, Poirot. Case solved.'

'You think this is amusing?' he asked dangerously.

'I think it's hilarious.'

'You have spent five months keeping to yourself, always using the excuse you are too tired to join me in anything—'

'I *have* been too tired. It's taken me all this time to feel like my old self.'

'I let it go because I knew you were recovering from the birth and adjusting to motherhood,' he continued as if she hadn't just interrupted him. 'And then I come home from a stressful trip and find you half-dressed and laughing with another man.'

'I was in a swimsuit and he's not another man. He's Mateo. And I think it's hilarious that you think a fit eighteen-year-old lad is going to flirt with a frumpy nearly twenty-five-year-old woman with a post-baby belly.'

'I don't know the meaning of the word frumpy but by your tone I assume it is not complimentary, so let me assure you: you are not frumpy. Post-baby belly or not, you are an attractive young woman. An attractive, *rich* young woman.'

Flora gritted her teeth to hide the spear of pain that shot through her chest at his qualifying her attractiveness.

She wished so hard her senses didn't bound with delight to be so close to him. Even with all the tension and anger simmering between them, her skin was buzzing and her heart thumping painfully.

'Mateo has been helping me learn Spanish,' she informed him icily. 'I've got no friends in this country, and Benjamin's too young for me to leave and visit my brother...'

The tightness of his features at this only enraged her more.

Justin, who'd been living in her London house since his return to England, was a subject Flora and Ramos never spoke of. Not that they spoke much about anything other than their son.

'I have already given you my word I won't let Benjamin have anything to do with him,' she said, trying hard to keep her tone moderate. It had been a promise that had broken her heart to make. 'I'm not going to take him with me to England, but there's no way Justin's stepping foot in Spain—he's convinced you'll set a hitman on him or something—so I'm basically alone here. Mateo's the only member of your staff willing to have a conversation with me. The rest treat me like a houseguest. They don't consult me about *anything*. Even my bodyguards answer me with grunts. You know damn well I'm not having an affair because they all watch me and report back to you, and how you have the nerve to get all macho and possessive about the possibility of me having one, even though the idea is preposterous, is pathetic.'

Ramos's sensuous lips pulled into a taut line before he smiled tightly. 'Why is the idea preposterous?' he asked silkily.

Flora rolled her eyes. 'Why do you think?'

His eyes glittered. 'Spell it out to me.'

Jutting her chin, trying hard to adopt her own poker face, she pointed at her post-baby belly.

His gaze drifted down to it then back to her face. He shrugged. 'I don't know what you're seeing but it is not what I see. You are as beautiful as you have always been. More so now. But I will tell you why I have the nerve to be macho and possessive about you having an affair and that's because you are my wife.'

'Your wife in name only,' she hit back, her brief flare of happiness that he'd called her beautiful doused with fury at his double standards. 'I don't want to have an affair but I don't see why I'm expected to stay home all chaste and pure when you can take all the mistresses and lovers that you like.'

His eyes narrowed. 'Oh, I can, can I?'

'There is nothing to stop you doing whatever you like and sleeping with whoever you like.' She folded her arms across her chest and tucked her hands into her sides so he couldn't see the tremors in them. 'But while we're on the subject I might as well ask you to show some discretion in your affairs—one day Benjamin will be old enough to read and he might find it upsetting to find details of his father's sex life splashed everywhere like happened with Aimee and all the others before her.'

Proud that she had managed to say all this without her voice choking, Flora forced herself to maintain eye contact with him.

But it was hard. There was something swirling in those melting depths, more than the toxic anger shrouding them, but she couldn't decipher its meaning.

A long period of dangerously uncomfortable silence ended when he coolly clarified, 'You are comfortable for me to have lovers?'

'Absolutely.' She wished that weren't a lie. 'Fill your boots.'

'You wouldn't find it upsetting?'

'Why would I?' she challenged.

'You don't want your husband to be faithful to you?'

'If I was married to a man I loved and had a proper marriage then of course, but even if we did have a proper marriage, I'm not naïve. Leopards can't change their spots. Some men are incapable of being faithful and you're one of them.'

His features darkened but his tone remained coolly moderate. 'You seem quite the expert on me.'

'An expert on men's infidelities. My dad's a serial philanderer, Justin too.'

Flora had been a baby when her mum had kicked her dad out. She'd been the same age as Benjamin was now. How her poor mum must have suffered, discovering her husband in bed with another woman, a much younger woman just to add insult to injury. She'd never bad-mouthed him to Flora but the fact she'd never dated again proved how damaging it had been to her. It pained Flora to acknowledge that, in this one respect, Justin was just like their father…or, he had been. Since his release from prison he'd lived quietly and, at her urging, joined Gamblers Anonymous.

Ramos steepled his fingers together. 'Let me see if I am understanding you correctly. Your father and brother are cheats, so therefore I am a cheat too?'

'Oh, come on.' She forced a laugh. The last thing she wanted was for him to think she cared what he did or who he did it with, but, as she'd learned, Ramos was far more observant than she'd ever given him credit for. She couldn't bear to think of him knowing how much it shredded her insides to imagine him with other women. 'I've been on the periphery of your life since I was a kid. Justin never mentioned you with the same woman twice. I never saw you with the same woman twice.'

Blonde Miranda again floated into her mind. And the women on his yacht and all the other women photographed with him she'd seen before she'd trained herself only to use social media for work purposes. And the women at his birthday pool party that she'd stupidly let her mother talk her into going to.

She pushed away the images she'd always reacted so violently to and prayed it didn't show on her face.

'I have had many lovers, I do not deny that and I will not apologise for it, but I have never lied and I have never cheated,' he stated flatly.

'You told me your mistresses always knew you wouldn't be faithful to them, that it defeated the purpose of *having* a mistress.'

'There was no cheating because that's not how the arrangements worked. My father cheated on my mother, many times. I know first-hand the damage affairs can do and, quite frankly, I find it insulting that you assume I'm like that.'

'If I have insulted you then I apologise,' she said stiffly. 'That was not my intention.'

'I would consider accepting your apology if I believed it, but I thank you for allowing me to *fill my boots* with whoever catches my eye. I will bear your open-minded generosity in mind.'

'You do that.'

'I will. Me however…' He shook his head, the flashing of his eye belying the moderacy of his voice. 'My own mind is a little less open and my generosity does not extend to permitting you the same.'

Flora's mouth fell open before she found her own voice. '*Permitting* me? Who are you to permit me to do anything?'

His nostrils flared. She could sense his temper hanging by a thread.

'Your husband, that's what I am, and, in case you need reminding, there is no statute of limitations on Hillier's crime in Monte Cleure. I can have the case against him re-opened and prosecuted whenever I so desire.'

Words uttered five months ago floated in her head. *Be nice to me and I can be very generous.*

'Are you threatening me?'

'I never make threats, *querida*. Only promises. Consider it a warning.'

'Okay, well, consider *this* a warning…' Leaning forwards, Flora looked deep into the molten eyes glimmering with fire and ice. 'All the money you've given me is sitting in an English bank account that you can't touch, doing nothing but accrue interest until the day I need it. There's more than enough in there to pay for the best legal representation for Justin to fight you every inch of the way.'

CHAPTER SIX

FLORA BRACED HERSELF for the explosion of rage that was sure to follow her threat in using Ramos's own money against him.

His generosity as a husband could not be faulted. The allowance she was given had allowed Flora to pay off her mortgage and the bank loan she'd taken for Justin's legal fees. Other than clothes and toiletries, she spent nothing on herself and was growing a nice nest egg.

She had no idea how long she awaited the explosion. So many emotions flickered over his face that they passed like a blur, the only unyielding feature the darkness of his eyes fixed tightly on hers.

The last thing she expected was the low chuckle that escaped from his widening mouth.

He settled back in his chair, folded his arms across his broad chest and shook his head. 'You really are back to your old self,' he murmured appreciatively. 'I had seen the changes...' He raised a shoulder. 'I had hoped.'

Taken aback at his change in demeanour and at something that was delivered sounding like a compliment, Flora was completely unable to think up a response.

'I knew recovering from birth could take some time but I didn't expect it to take quite so long for the Flora Hillier I have known all these years to come back to life.' With a subtle wink, he added, 'Let us hope it never comes to my money paying for both the prosecution and the defence, eh?'

'Well...quite.'

Eyes now gleaming, Ramos straightened and flexed his fingers. 'Correct me if I am misunderstanding you, but you are unhappy with how my staff treat you?'

Now confused at the change of conversational direction, she nodded and cleared her throat. 'They treat me like a houseguest. Apart from Mateo, who doesn't flirt with me but does treat me as a human being deserving respect,' she felt compelled to add.

He touched his fingers to his forehead. 'I apologise for misreading the situation.'

She thought her eyes might pop out in shock. 'You do?'

'I do.' His lips pulled into a grimace. 'It has been a difficult few weeks.'

'Why's that?'

His dark eyes held hers. 'I have a family now. I felt the distance. The first thing I saw when I arrived home was my beautiful wife, who I have not seen laugh since she moved here, laughing with a good-looking young man.' He raised his shoulders. 'I should not have jumped to conclusions.'

And her heart shouldn't be leaping that Ramos had called her beautiful again and had practically admitted to jealousy. Or possessiveness. Or something along those lines.

Most likely any possessiveness on his part came from her bearing the title of his wife. It was his arrogant pride that was possessive.

'Now, am I right in thinking you want the staff to treat you as the mistress of the house?' he said in a lighter tone.

That knocked the confused thoughts out of her, and she blanched. If she never heard the word mistress again it would be too soon. 'I want them to respect me as your wife.'

His gaze held hers for a time that stretched so long Flora found herself holding her breath again and fighting not to lose herself in the melting swirl.

'They do respect you, *querida*,' he said.

'They spy on me,' she whispered.

'They watch you, yes,' he agreed. 'On my instructions. But it is not easy for them to respect you as my wife when you do not act as my wife. A marriage is the union of two people and so far there has been no unity between us. I blame myself for that—I should never have put you in this guest room. I only put you in here because you were fragile from the birth and needed time to recover and adjust to our new life, but I see now that was a mistake. It allowed you to hide away. I was trying to do the right thing by you but that time allowed too much separation between us and caused much distrust, as what just happened testifies.'

'But there hasn't ever been trust between us,' she replied shakily. Dizzying heat was filling her head at the direction in which she could sense Ramos was taking them.

'Then it is time for us to build some, if only for our son's sake, and time for us to build a proper marriage.'

Her mouth ran dry. The thuds of her heart deepened with a violence that matched the churning in her stomach. 'What do you mean?'

But she knew.

Ramos stretched an arm and took hold of her left hand. Turning it palm up, he traced a circle over the sensitive skin.

Flora was helpless to stop the shiver that rippled through her at the sensation.

He shifted closer, his knee now pressing against hers, and traced the length of her wedding finger. His velvet voice dropped to a murmur that was as seductive as the melting swirl in his eyes. 'You are my wife and I am your husband, and it is time for us to build a real marriage together with you in my bed and my ring on your finger.'

His scent was filling her senses. Memories of the night they'd shared were clamouring for release and, though she fought desperately to contain them, she couldn't contain the remembered caresses of his hands and mouth. They sprang so vividly she could feel the sensation of them on her skin, powerful enough to send a pulse throbbing deep in her pelvis and bring her hurling to her senses.

She snatched her hand away and shoved her chair back, far out of his reach.

Horribly aware that she'd been a whisker from falling under his spell again, painfully aware that her face was crimson, she managed to say with just the right amount of indignation, 'Excuse *me*, but you can't just suddenly demand I share a bed with you.'

Far from being perturbed, he appraised her with a knowing smile. 'I demand nothing, but you made your choice when you signed our wedding certificate. You signed up for marriage without caveats, and so did I.'

'That doesn't mean you can just take your conjugal rights now you deem me well enough for it!'

'Who said anything about conjugal rights?' he asked innocently. 'I merely said you would be sharing my room and my bed, nothing more than that.' He rose to his feet and winked. 'I'm sure you'll agree though that sharing a bed should help kill the irrational jealousy we both seem to suffer from.'

'I'm certainly not jealous!' she spluttered. Where on earth had he got that idea from? Hadn't she just practically given him carte blanche to have all the affairs he wanted? Would an irrationally jealous person do that?

He raised a disbelieving brow then said, 'We will choose a ring tomorrow but everything else changes from now. I will instruct Madeline to move your possessions into my room when we go out tonight.'

'Out?' she echoed.

His eyes pulsed. 'Yes, *querida*. Out. On a date. Just me and my beautiful wife. I have let you hide away for too long, from me and from the world.'

Then, with long, languid strides, he disappeared from her room, leaving Flora shell-shocked from all the grenades he'd just detonated and the palm of her hand still tingling manically from where his fingers had caressed it.

* * *

In her five months living in Barcelona, Flora had never left the villa without her son and it was with a huge dose of trepidation that she kissed his sleeping face goodnight.

It was with even greater trepidation that she stepped onto the galleried landing. From her vantage point she could see Ramos waiting for her on one of the deep blue velvet sofas in the living area. Dressed in a snazzy navy suit with a black open-necked shirt, his ankle hooked over his thigh, he had a glass of bourbon in one hand and was reading something on his phone with the other.

Her breath caught in her throat, the thuds of her heart echoing loudly in her ears.

He really was the most beautiful man alive, from the top of his cropped dark hair to the tips of his long toes. There was not a part of her that didn't long for him, and not just a longing to punch him.

God help her, how was she supposed to share a bed with him without losing her mind?

Her shell shock from his grenades had slowly worn off, leaving her dazed at how easily he was able to turn any situation to his advantage. It would be impressive if she weren't the one in the firing line of his sharp brain.

Gripping tightly on the glass balustrade, she remembered begging him to slow down when he first demanded she marry him. By that point he'd probably mapped out their whole future in his head.

When Ramos made up his mind to do something, he wanted it done yesterday. She could hardly believe he'd waited five whole months to make her share the marital bedroom, not if his intention really had been to move her into it from the start.

One minute they'd been arguing about his irrational jealousy over Mateo—though why he'd accused her of suffering from irrational jealousy too, she didn't know, the idea was ridiculous—the next her whole idea about their marriage was being upended and decided on.

Emotionally, her recovery *had* taken a long time. She'd given birth to the most precious child in the world and had felt the loss of her mother, who would never meet her grandson, as keenly as when she'd first died. Ramos had sensed this, she realised. Impulsive and vengeful he might be, but he was also capable of empathy and that only made her heart swell even more for him. Only added to the danger she was in.

Flora wasn't like his other lovers. She could never be like them. She just wasn't made that way. As an adolescent, she'd hated the way Ramos and her brother treated women, feeling it too much like the way her father treated them. Gradually though, she'd learned the women they went with were of the same mindset. They were women who didn't care for commitment either.

Now she was even less like those other women. She'd had a child. Her body bore the evidence of it and would for the rest of her life.

Her father had cheated on her mother in the aftermath of both her pregnancies with younger women whose bodies were lithe and perfect. And her father had supposedly loved her mother! How could Flora's body not repulse Ramos?

She couldn't allow there to be intimacy between them. She just couldn't.

She didn't dare.

As if sensing her gaze on him, he raised his stare to her and the swelling of her heart almost choked her.

He met her at the bottom of the stairs, hooded eyes drifting over her, taking everything in.

'You look beautiful,' he said simply.

Blushing furiously at the compliment, she shrugged and strove for lightness. 'It took me long enough.'

Tonight, she'd chosen a black dress with red polka dots that had a kimono-style neck and short sleeves, and a puffed-out skirt that disguised her bum and hips. She'd held her breath when Madeline did the zip up for her, certain it would get stuck halfway up her back, but it had fastened easily. For her feet she'd selected a pair of elegant black pointed shoes with only a small heel, and twisted her chestnut hair into a loose chignon.

He chuckled. 'It has been a long time since you last went out?'

'My last date was with a midwife, so yes.'

'Then I hope you find this evening makes up for all you have missed out on.'

'Where are we going?' When she'd sought him out earlier to ask him, he'd refused to tell her, saying only that she should dress up.

His mouth widened into that devastating smile. 'For dinner and then the ballet.'

Flora turned her head for one last glimpse of the villa as the driver left Ramos's grounds.

'He will be fine,' Ramos said, reading her mind. 'Madeline has three children of her own and eight grandchildren.'

'I know,' she sighed. 'It's just that I've never left him before.'

'He won't even know we have gone,' he promised. 'And we'll only be a fifteen-minute drive away. Now tell me, have you seen *Giselle* before?'

'Yes.'

He grinned. 'How many times?'

'Only three. What about you?'

'I've never been to the ballet in my life.'

'Why not?'

He shrugged. 'Never thought it would be my thing.'

'Then why take me there?'

'Because I know how much you enjoy it.' His phone rang. He pulled it out of his suit jacket pocket and sighed. 'My Vegas lawyer. My apologies. I left before we could get everything wrapped up. Let me take this and then I'll turn it off.'

While he took his call, Flora gazed out of the window at the late summer sun fading to a pink ember on the horizon, and thought back to the time he'd bought her tickets to the ballet before.

It had been a present for her twenty-first birthday.

She hadn't expected a gift from him as he'd offered to host the party in one of his Mayfair hotel casino's function rooms free of charge. She hadn't wanted to accept his generous offer or invite him to it, but her mum had been recently diagnosed with cancer and her mum considered Ramos a second son. So she'd felt obliged.

She'd been obliged to kiss his cheek in greeting, as she had everyone else too, when he'd arrived with her brother. Her lungs had filled with the spicy scent she so hated.

Hated because it was wonderful. It was one of the many things she'd hated about him as an adolescent; hated the near-constant urge to trail in his wake and sniff him.

She could smell it now. Every inhalation came with a dose of his scent.

She remembered how her friends had flocked to him like a pack of gulls around a discarded sandwich. She'd wanted to smack the lot of them, something that had *really* disturbed her.

And she remembered catching his eye from the other side of the function room. He'd been in mid-conversation with her brother and he'd cut himself off from whatever he'd been saying and just stared at her. It was the first time in her life Flora had met Ramos's stare and held it…held it because she'd been unable to drag her gaze away. She'd been trapped. That awful sticky sensation had crashed through her, her breaths shallowing to nothing.

For all she knew, she might still be there now, spellbound in his gaze, if her friend Molly hadn't thrust a drink in her hand.

He'd approached her a short while later and asked her to dance.

The excitement that had thrummed through her veins and the rapid pounding of her heart…she'd never experienced anything like it. It had been the single most frightening moment of her life, and she'd danced stiffly and held her breath to stop his spicy scent filling her lungs for the entire song, then walked away without a word, all without looking into his eyes. She'd known she must never make that mistake again. Never.

In the morning, the day of her actual birthday, there had been a knock on the door of the suite Ramos had put her and her mum in. A bellboy had handed the gift box to her with birthday wishes from the owner. In the box had lain tickets for that evening's performance of *Cinderella* in Paris. Included were first-class return flight tickets for her and her mum, and a note stating a suite had been reserved under her name in his Parisian hotel.

His generosity had thrilled her mum but terrified Flora, who'd still been able to feel the imprint of his arms around her from when they'd danced. It had been a generosity that couldn't go unacknowledged though, and she'd handwritten a short letter from her Parisian suite after the performance, thanking him.

'I have been thinking,' Ramos said, breaking through the memories and putting his phone back in his pocket, 'and now that you are rejoining the world, it is time for us to employ a nanny. Madeline is happy to babysit for us tonight but she has her own family and it is not fair to expect her to extend her duties.'

'Getting a nanny seems a bit excessive for just the odd night out,' she said doubtfully. Flora had only been comfortable leaving Benjamin in the housekeeper's care because Benjamin was comfortable with her and, for all that Flora had issues with Madeline, she didn't doubt she would look after her baby as well as she would her own flesh and blood.

'It will be more than the odd night out and it will make life easier to have someone on site. I am thinking of you too. I know you haven't said anything about starting your business up again, but I remember how much you got from it and if you feel you want to start it up again at some point in the future—we can turn one of the guest rooms into a studio for you—then you won't have to worry about him.'

She met his stare, wishing her heart weren't swelling again for him.

Flora ran a small business from the home she'd bought herself with her share of her mother's inheritance, designing and creating bespoke embroidery patches that could be ironed onto clothing and creating embroidery prints from clients' photographs. Her website currently informed potential customers that she was taking a sabbatical.

Since Benjamin's birth she felt that all her creativity had deserted her and she'd hardly given any thought to starting up again. But Ramos had. Already that sharp brain was thinking ahead to the day she might feel ready to give her creativity an outlet and was making plans to accommodate it for her.

Oh, how could one man have so many different facets to him? Thoughtfulness and empathy versus vengefulness and cruelty. How masochistic was she to wish for him to show more of the vengefulness and cruelty to her because those were the traits that made it easier to dislike him?

But they had never stopped her wanting him, had they? His abhorrent treatment of her after their night together hadn't stopped her dreaming of him. Hadn't stopped the constant ache in her chest.

The car came to a stop.

They'd arrived at the opera house.

CHAPTER SEVEN

THE RESTAURANTS IN and around the opera house were heaving with people dining and drinking before the evening's performance. Ramos led her past them all and through to a nondescript, narrow side street that looked as if its better days were centuries ago.

Flora wrinkled her nose at the peeling door of the terraced house he knocked on.

He caught her expression and winked.

The door was opened by a tiny, wizened old man who greeted them both as if they were his long-lost children. Not understanding a word he said, a bemused Flora followed Ramos's lead and stepped inside. And then she gasped.

This must have been how the kids felt when they opened the wardrobe door into Narnia.

The whole street must have been knocked into one vast building to create this magnificent space.

Glass tables were strategically placed around an elaborate glass water fountain, all of which were underlit with burnished orange lights that cast the restaurant in a golden glow that managed to be opulent and showy without being gaudy. The trickling from the fountain perfectly complemented the low-level background music and hum of conversation. As they walked the quietly busy room to their table, their silhouettes cast shadows along the walls.

'What is this place?' she whispered.

'The best kept secret in Barcelona,' he murmured, leaning down to speak into the top of her hair.

With the warmth of his breath soaking through her skull, Flora gratefully took her seat.

Menus were placed before them with a flourish. There was the grand total of one item for each course displayed on it.

'We have the performance to watch soon so are eating from the quick menu,' Ramos explained. 'It just tells us what we are going to be served with. If you like it here, we can make a night of it another time soon—

they do a twelve-course tasting menu that changes daily and is always excellent.'

A bottle of white wine was brought to their table. Flora allowed the waiter to pour her only a small amount. She'd never been much of a drinker even before she found out she was pregnant. She took a small sip of it and then their first course of almond gazpacho was placed in front of them. It was so fresh and silky smooth she would have gladly buried her face in it. All too soon her bowl was empty and all that was left were tiny crumbs of the fluffy warm roll it had been served with.

Relaxing into the luxurious environment, she took another tiny sip of wine and said, 'What you were saying about hiring a nanny... Knowing you, your mind is already made up...'

He grinned at her observation.

'But I'm happy to go along with it on condition that I'm involved in the hiring process.'

'That is as it should be. What kind of person do you have in mind?'

'Just someone nice. And preferably young. Someone who could be a friend.'

His eyes narrowed a touch.

Uh oh. That meant he was thinking.

'A word of advice,' he said. 'Whoever we choose, don't get too close.'

'What do you mean?'

'You will be their employer. Mixing business with pleasure is a recipe for disaster. Now that you are coming out into the world you will make friends. We have been invited to a party on Saturday night. You will meet people there. Many of my friends have young children—'

'Do they?' she asked, surprised. Ramos and Justin's circle of friends had been kindred spirits to them, hedonistic party animals.

He obviously guessed what she was thinking for he drily said, 'People do grow up, you know.'

'Not everyone does. My father never has. He's still the same pound shop playboy he's always been.'

'My father too…although he is more of a yacht shop playboy,' he added with a wry smile as their next course of pork tenderloin was presented to them.

'Am I ever going to meet him?' she asked, cutting through her pork as easily as if slicing through butter.

'When he finishes his latest holiday,' Ramos said.

'He's been on holiday for five months?'

'He has a new wife.'

'Really? Since when?'

'A few weeks after we married. She's your age.'

'You never said.'

'She's his fourth wife since my mother died. It won't last. They never do.'

Unsure how she was supposed to respond to this, Flora decided silence would prevent her from saying the wrong thing, and popped a cube of jellied apple into her mouth. A taste sensation exploded on her tongue.

'He's retired and has a few billion in the bank,' he explained. 'What better way to spend it than with the latest model of your preferred type of woman?'

A roll of nausea sloshed through her belly as she imagined herself years from now—a few years maybe, or maybe longer—pushed aside for a younger, prettier version of herself.

But she could only be pushed aside if she became his lover as well as his wife.

'Isn't he even curious about meeting his grandson?' she asked.

'Oh, I'm sure he's curious. Just not curious enough. I told you before—he's selfish. He's always been selfish but age has made him worse. Once I came of age he decided his presence in my life was no longer required and has done exactly as he pleases since.'

Whispers of a remembered conversation floated in her head and before she could stop herself Flora blurted out, 'He went to Martinique.'

'Sorry?' he asked.

'Your father. Years ago. Justin invited me to stay at yours for the weekend but Mum would only let me go if you weren't there—she loved you to pieces but she knew when you and Justin got together, trouble followed. You were supposed to spend the weekend with your dad in Barcelona but when you got there he'd flown off to Martinique instead so you came back to Oxford.' And hooked up with a lady friend.

He simply stared at her.

'What?' she asked.

'That must have been ten years ago.'

'Eleven. Nearly twelve,' she added help-fully.

A slow smile spread across his face. 'That is some memory you have.'

No way was she admitting why that particular weekend had stuck in her memory so she gave another shrug, and hoped it covered the disquiet racing through her as, for the first time, she considered that Ramos's father had stood him up that weekend. His own father.

'Was a lady involved in Martinique?' she asked in the same light tone, being careful to sound conversational rather than probing.

'With my father, there's always a lady involved,' he answered wryly. 'My mother never trusted him not to stray—when I was a child she always insisted we travel with him.'

'Did that stop him?'

'I don't know. His opportunities to stray were limited.'

'Why did she stay if she thought he would cheat?'

'For me.' He raised a shoulder. 'She believed children do better living with both their parents and she was right. We had a good life together, the three of us.'

She caught a momentary trace of wistfulness on his face and gently forked her last croquette to stop herself from extending a comforting hand to him.

'I'm sorry you lost her so young,' she said quietly. 'That must have been devastating.'

Losing her mother at twenty-two had been devastating, but trying to imagine going through that at the age of ten when the worst nightmare she'd ever had was of being in a department store and losing sight of her mum, a dream she'd woken from sobbing... It would have ripped the soul from her.

'It was.' His eyes narrowed and flashed. 'But it toughened me up. When you lose the person you love most in the world at a young age, you learn that nothing can beat that. Nothing. There can be no greater pain. The worst thing that can happen to you has happened. There is nothing left to fear and nothing can hurt you again.'

Flora's throat had closed up and she had to work hard to open it enough to swallow her last mouthful.

Ramos took another drink of his wine then bestowed her with the devilishly handsome smile she hated and adored in equal measure. 'Seeing as the show will start soon, why don't you tell me the storyline so I can know what's going on?'

She knew a deliberate change of subject when she heard one, and she was grateful for it. Imagining Ramos as a vulnerable, heartbroken boy filled her with too much compassion for him.

The seats Ramos had got for them were in a private box. It was clearly one of the theatre's most exclusive boxes as they had their own bar and a private usher to cater to all their whims and needs throughout the performance. The usher hung Ramos's jacket up for him and poured them a drink each before bowing his head and slipping out of the box.

If they needed him, they had only to press a button and he would come running.

'Is this yours?' Flora asked, delighted with such an excellent, unrestricted view of the stage, but with a stomach full of knots at the intimate space they would share for the next few hours.

They would be sharing a much more intimate space when they returned home, a thought that only tightened the knots.

'No. A friend's.' He sat next to her and stretched his long legs out. 'But, as I know how much you enjoy all theatre productions, I have set the ball rolling for a box of our own.'

Her eyes widened in disbelief. 'Are you serious?'

He gave a wolfish grin. 'Always. Did I not tell you I could be generous?'

Overwhelmed that a man she knew cared nothing for the theatre was preparing himself for a future of plentiful theatre visits, she gazed at the handsome face, at the straight patrician nose and the closely shaved jaw and felt something in her heart sigh...

An alarm went off in her brain and she

quickly pulled herself together to drily say, 'Generosity is your middle name, Ramos.'

And it was, she realised. Ramos had an intrinsically generous nature, not just with his money but with his time too.

'It is,' he agreed smugly, 'and I have told you many times to call me Alejandro.'

She adopted her most innocent face. 'Sorry. I occasionally suffer from amnesia.'

The roar of laughter that burst from his mouth had the audience below craning their necks.

The auditorium lights dimmed. The brief flare of shared amusement dimmed with it.

Settling back in her seat, Flora crossed her legs away from him and folded her arms across her chest so there was no danger of any part of their bodies touching. Mercifully, the seats in the box were much larger than ordinary seats.

The lights on the stage went up. The orchestra played its first beat.

Flora took a deep breath, fixed her stare on the stage and waited for the magic to transport her.

But the magic never came.

Here, in the privacy of their darkened box, she was far too aware of Ramos for anything else to properly penetrate. The distance she'd put between them was too slight to be effective.

As the first act went on, the awareness prickling over her skin deepened. Slowly but surely, he leaned closer to her. If not for the armrest separating them, their arms and thighs would be touching and it was taking everything she had to hold her position, keep her eyes glued to the stage and not move so much as a fraction of her body. Pretend she couldn't feel the burn of his stare on her.

And yet, although the dancing itself passed in a blur, the sweeping music seeped into her, and as the end of the first act approached she could feel the madness of a betrayed, heartbroken Giselle in the pounding beats of her heart…

They were the same pounding beats that had bruised her chest when she'd realised Ramos had severed himself from her, and she knew beyond a shadow of a doubt that if she succumbed to the desire that burned so deep inside her for him, her heart would once again open like a flower and leave her vulnerable to being hurt again.

When the lights came up for the interval she held her position a moment longer before facing him.

He hadn't moved. His melting eyes gleamed and a knowing smile played on his lips. 'Enjoying it?' he asked lazily.

She pulled a wide smile on her face. 'It's great. What about you?'

He raised the shoulder furthest from her. 'I will have to watch it again.'

'Why?'

He dipped his face a little closer. 'Because I have been watching you.'

The sticky heat of arousal rushed through her again, and she reflexively tightened the cross of her legs.

Thank God the usher chose that moment to enter their box.

Flora snatched at the opportunity and fled to the sanctuary of the ladies' bathroom.

The ladies itself was a plush, intimate space for the female occupants of the private boxes and had an array of toiletries and cosmetics for patrons to use. Spotting a cooling mist, Flora pulled the front of her dress out and sprayed the mist between her cleavage. Too late she noticed its seductive scent and almost stamped her feet to curse herself.

Ramos would probably assume she'd sprayed it for his benefit.

She dawdled returning to the box and then avoided conversation with him by keeping the usher busy making her a variety of mocktails to enjoy. She managed to play the charade right until the lights dimmed again.

Retaking her seat, Flora determined that in this, the second act, she would tune him out properly.

Her resolve lasted as long as it took for the first dancer to enter the stage.

This time, not even the music penetrated. Ramos didn't stare at her. No, he leaned his head right against hers so they were a whisker from touching. His soft hair tickled her forehead. His spicy scent floated in and out of her airwaves. His arm rested on the barrier between them, his long fingers hanging over her side of it. She tightened her arms around her chest and buried her hands in her sides so her tingling fingers couldn't reach for them. She crossed her legs so tightly that she wouldn't be surprised if she cut off her blood supply.

But nothing she did worked to stop the assault on her body from the man who wasn't even touching her.

'Querida?' he whispered after she'd sat frozen for what felt like fifteen hours.

She had to swallow hard to reply. 'What?'

'You need to breathe.'

Her face turned to him before she could stop herself making the movement.

The tips of their noses made contact.

She was breathing now. Shallow, ragged breaths.

She was helpless to stop her eyes lifting to meet his gaze, shadowed in the darkness but still filled with that hooded, hypnotic power that so easily caught her in its trap.

A finger brushed lightly over her cheekbone.

His breath was warm against her tingling lips.

She was locked in his hooded and, oh, so seductive stare; the cavity in her chest filled, a swelling that pushed into her throat making it impossible to speak…impossible to pull away.

The finger drifted down her neck and then skimmed back up to take gentle hold of her chin. Her heart was thumping so hard she thought…

His lips fused against hers and sucked out any thoughts she had.

Languidly, his mouth moved…and hers moved with equal languidness. Their lips parted slowly as his hand cupped her cheek tenderly.

The tip of his tongue darted against hers.

A moan echoed in her ears… It came from her.

With the same torturously slow pace, the kiss deepened. Slowly, his fingers tiptoed to her ear and traced the contours, burning her with shivers of delight, then dipped behind to thread into her hair…

A loud burst of applause cut through the sensory pleasure.

In an instant, Flora yanked her hand from the nape of his neck—when had she put that there?—pushed at Ramos's chest and jumped to her feet.

She clapped and cheered and hollered until her hands were raw and her throat hoarse.

Flora kept her arms firmly crossed on the short walk back to their waiting car.

She couldn't believe she'd let him kiss her.

She couldn't believe she'd kissed him back.

What was *wrong* with her? Had she taken leave of her senses? She must have done.

In the back of the car, she huddled herself against the door, trying to create as much distance from Ramos as she could.

She could still taste him on her tongue. Her lips still tingled manically. The hot, sticky sensation…it still simmered in waves.

'Something troubling you, *querida*?' he asked lightly.

'No… Yes!' Taking a deep breath, she faced him. 'That was a mistake.'

'What was?'

'You know what.'

He pulled an innocent face. 'The ballet?'

'Stop playing games,' she cried. 'Our kiss.'

His eyes gleamed. 'Ah, *that*.'

'Yes, that. I don't want you getting the wrong idea.'

He leaned his face closer and dropped his voice to a husky drawl. 'Are you trying to tell me that I shouldn't build my hopes up and expect you to throw yourself into my arms the minute the bedroom door is closed?'

Her skin danced just to imagine it. 'Exactly.'

'Then consider your message understood.'

'Thank you.'

'What we do in our bed will be up to you. If you wish to do nothing but sleep beside me then that is your right and I will respect your wishes.' Nostrils flaring, he shifted ever closer so that his cheek was a tissue away from touching hers and whispered, 'But just think, what we found the night we spent together… We can have that again, *querida*. And more. Much more.'

CHAPTER EIGHT

THE BEATS OF Flora's heart were weighty as she climbed the villa's stairs, Ramos close behind her.

His bedroom door loomed large.

Her bedroom door now.

Theirs.

She swallowed. 'I'm going to check on Benjamin.'

Not waiting for a response, she opened the door opposite and tiptoed to the cot that had pride of place next to the king-size bed Benjamin would one day upgrade to.

He was fast asleep.

The urge to lift him into her arms and hold his comforting, solid weight to her chest was almost overwhelming but, knowing it would be pure selfishness to wake him, she settled for lightly stroking his soft hair.

She couldn't use her son as a human shield

against his father... No, not his father, she admitted painfully, but herself.

Benjamin's cherubic sleeping face reminded her that she'd found the strength needed to carry her through a time when she could have easily crumbled under the weight of her fears and worries. In comparison to that time, sharing a bed with Ramos was trifling. Even if it didn't feel trifling.

All she needed was to find her zen.

Breathing deeply and slowly, she willed her mind into a state of calm.

Only when her heart had slowed to a vaguely regular beat did she leave the nursery, filled with resolve that she could act and behave as if sharing a bed with her husband meant nothing more than the sleepovers she'd had with her school friends.

She entered the room her son had been conceived in for the first time since his conception. There was no sign of his father.

'Ramos?' she called out.

'In the bathroom,' he called back.

She remembered his majestic bathroom suite all too well. They'd shared a shower before he'd given her a lift to her hotel and asked if he could see her again that night.

She walked as far as the archway that led into it and, without actually looking into it, said, 'Where's my stuff been put?'

Seconds later, Ramos's towering figure appeared wearing only a dark blue towel around his snake hips.

Her zen practically flew out of the window.

Painfully aware her cheeks were burning with colour, Flora took a hasty step back and averted her eyes from the muscular bronzed torso that had plagued her thoughts every night before she drifted into sleep for years.

A gleam flickered in his eyes before he inclined his head. 'I will show you.'

With long, languid strides, he led her past the humongous bed, the tight muscles of his buttocks clearly outlined beneath the towel. She only just managed to avert her eyes when he stopped at an archway and turned to her.

He swept an elegant arc. 'Your dressing room.'

Flora had thought her last dressing room

was big. This one could rival a department store…okay, a slight exaggeration. But, still, wow.

'I'm going to take a shower,' Ramos informed her. 'So I will leave you to it…unless you wish to join me?'

She answered with a glare that had him sauntering off chuckling.

Managing to stop herself ogling his backside again by a breath, Flora dragged the heavy drape across its rail to give herself privacy, but, instead of changing into her pyjamas, sat on the red velvet chaise longue and buried her face in her hands.

So much for her zen.

Why, oh, why had she kissed him? Her awareness of him had been bad enough before but now it was all a hundred times worse.

After changing into her pyjamas, she hung around in her dressing room until she was certain he'd left the bathroom and had had time to get into bed.

She counted to ten then darted across the room, not looking at him.

The first section of the bathroom suite

had vanity units running along opposite side walls. Her toiletries had been placed neatly on one of them and she cleaned her face and brushed her teeth, then brushed her hair, dragging out the process as long as she could and searching desperately for her zen.

Ramos, lying on his side of the bed staring up at the ceiling, turned his face at the sound of her footsteps. 'Did you find everything, *querida*?'

'Yes, thank you.' Cheered that she'd managed to sound normal, she lifted the sheets and slid under them.

The double emperor bed was so big she had acres of space to call her own. Ramos was far enough away that they could both stretch like starfish and not touch.

After they wished each other a polite goodnight, Ramos deactivated the lights.

It was one of the longest, most torturous nights of Flora's existence.

The sleep Flora had rediscovered had been snatched away from her again, this time by a six-foot-three hunk who slept nude in the same bed as her. Slept soundly. Three nights she'd lain awake burning inside, her mind consumed with the hunk beside her, knowing all she would have to do was prod him with a finger and he would wake up and put her out of her frustrated misery. And then her mind would go into overdrive imagining all the things he would do to her, pushing sleep even further away. After all that torture and the long days of his gregarious company, she now had to deal with the torture of sitting by his side on the leather sofa of his home office interviewing potential candidates for the role of nanny for their son. It was the closest they'd been in a physical sense since the night of the ballet.

'Which one did you prefer?' Ramos asked once the final interview was done, twisting to face her.

None of them.

They'd interviewed five women for the role. She had no idea how Ramos had been able to organise it all in such super-quick time but, as she had learned, when Ramos had an idea in his head he was single-minded until it was accomplished. Unfortunately the potential candidates made her feel a little like the children in *Mary Poppins* looking out of the window with dread at all the stern-faced women lined up, knowing one of them would be tasked with caring for them. Except none of the nannies they were interviewing were in the slightest bit stern-faced. On the contrary. They were all smiley, fresh-faced and, without exception, beautiful.

Flora hated herself for it, but her imagination ran riot whenever Ramos was away. How would she cope with a beautiful woman sleeping under their roof with them?

'They all seem nice,' she said truthfully.

Nice and smiley and young and beautiful and without a single stretchmark between them. Not one of them would look out of place on Ramos's yacht.

'You must have a favourite?' he said.

'Do you?'

'It doesn't matter what I think. They're all equally well qualified and all have impeccable references, but you are the one who will spend the most time with them so it should be your decision.'

She twisted her wedding ring they'd bought two days ago. She couldn't seem to stop herself from twisting it. Ramos had surprised her by buying himself a matching one. It was a public proclamation that he was a married man.

Oh, she was being *ridiculous*. Ramos wouldn't have an affair under his own roof. He just wouldn't, especially since she'd asked him to be discreet in his affairs.

Oh, *why* had she practically given him licence to sleep with whoever he wanted when the thought of Ramos with another woman had made her feel violently sick since she was thirteen and unwittingly caught that glimpse of him naked?

That made her straighten.

Oh, God, had she actually fancied him all that time? Was that what it had all been about? Had it all been jealousy?

No *way*. That was ridiculous. She'd felt *sorry* for all those women. The sickness in her stomach whenever she thought of them was empathy for the heartbreak she'd assumed was heading their way when Ramos quickly bored of them.

Liar...

'Are you okay, *querida*?'

Realising she'd fallen into a daze, Flora blinked and rubbed her arms and generally tried to look as if there were nothing wrong and that she hadn't just had a frightening epiphany.

'I was just considering the options,' she said quickly. 'And I'd like to employ Sinead.'

'The Irish one?'

'Yep. She seemed the nicest and friendliest of all of them.' The most genuine too.

'Just remember what I said about not getting too close. You will be her employer, not her friend.'

'Is it your experience with Justin that makes you say that?' It was a question that had played on her mind numerous times these last few days.

His features tightened but he gave a sharp nod. 'I gave him the job because he had the qualifications and he's damn good with numbers. I trusted him.'

The job in question had been Finance Director for the Ramos Group, the company Ramos formed when he graduated from university. His billionaire father had given him a huge sum of money as a graduation present, which Ramos had promptly used to purchase run-down properties in central city locations and convert them into his chain of hotel casinos. He'd brought Justin on board four years later and paid him handsomely for it.

'When the theft from my Athens casino was discovered and brought to my attention, Hillier was the last person I suspected. He told me someone must have hacked into his computer and stolen his passcodes and I believed him because we had been friends for thirteen years and I'd thought of him as a brother.'

Watching his face go through a contortion of emotions, she instinctively reached out a hand to cover the fist he'd made but pulled it back before making contact and held it tightly on her lap.

'He really hurt you, didn't he?' she said quietly.

His eyes flashed dangerously. 'No, *querida*, he didn't hurt me—nothing has had the power to hurt me since I was ten years old—but he did abuse my trust, and trust is not something I give easily.'

'But don't you miss him?' she probed, searching his handsome face intently.

'No.'

She didn't believe him. She only half believed him about Justin not hurting him, but no way did she believe that he didn't miss him.

'I think back on how close you two were…' She sighed. 'I was jealous of you.'

His brow rose. 'Jealous of what?'

'Your closeness. I thought you were stealing him from me,' she admitted. 'I was eleven when he went to university and I missed him terribly. I was so excited about his visits home and when he brought you back with him…' She shrugged. 'I hated you for stealing what I considered to be *my* precious time with him.'

'Is that why you always stuck your nose in the air around me?'

She smiled, remembering her skinny little self back then. 'I was used to it being just him and me…and Mum, of course.'

'And I was the interloper?'

'In my mind, yes. I was too young to think of what it must have meant for you to give up your weekends of wild partying on the student campus to stay in our little home.' Until that moment, it had never occurred to her what a big thing that must have been for an eighteen-year-old boy, and she gazed into his eyes, suddenly wishing she could go back thirteen years and welcome the motherless Spanish young man into her home with the same embracing generosity her mother had. 'You were generous with your time when Mum was ill too,' she whispered. All those visits that had brought such a smile to her mother's face.

His face inched closer to her. 'You are thinking maybe I am not so bad after all?'

'I learned that the day our son was born,' she whispered. 'I couldn't have got through it without you.'

Suddenly realising she was in danger of falling into his eyes again, Flora jumped up. 'Right, that's enough compliments for one day. Your head's big enough as it is—I don't want you getting stuck in the door. Do you want to call Sinead and tell her she has the job or shall I?'

'I will,' he said, following her lead and rising to his feet. 'You go and get yourself and Benjamin ready. I'm taking you shopping.'

'For what?'

'Clothes and jewellery for my beautiful wife's enrolment into my high society life, and if I am lucky she will let me spy on her in the dressing rooms.' Then he cupped her cheeks, planted a smacker of a kiss to her lips, and sauntered out of the office like a strutting peacock leaving Flora not knowing whether to laugh or cry.

Flora gazed out of her dressing room window the next day watching Ramos and Benjamin in the swimming pool. She couldn't hear Benjamin's happy squeals but could see them, and the joy on Ramos's face.

She'd been preparing to take Benjamin for a swim herself when Ramos had appeared in the nursery wearing only his swimming shorts and announced he'd be joining them.

As the thought of wearing a swimsuit around the man she lusted after with more desperation with each passing day, knowing most of her own body would be on show for him to sweep his expert eye over, made her feel as if she were coming out in hives, she'd quickly handed the change bag to him.

'Do some daddy-son bonding,' she'd told him brightly, relieved she hadn't changed into her own swimsuit at that point. 'I'll help Sinead get settled in.'

In typical Ramos fashion, he'd arranged for their new nanny to move in and start her employment immediately.

His returning stare had been scrutinising but he'd shrugged his broad shoulders and lifted Benjamin into his arms.

She was looking at those broad shoulders now. The strength in them. The smoothness of them. Ramos wasn't particularly vain—she supposed when you were God's gift to women you took your gorgeous face for granted—but he worked out. The end result was right there in the distance, and she soaked it up in a way she never did when alone in the room with him. The way she never *dared* to do when alone with him.

The muscles on his back bunched as he lifted Benjamin into the air.

Stop looking at him, she beseeched herself.

She might as well tell her heart to stop beating.

How much longer could she bear it?

Seeing him now, striding around in nothing but a pair of short swim-shorts, reminded her all too much of that night of his pool party.

She hadn't wanted to go. She'd turned down so many invitations from him. They'd all come after her twenty-first birthday, delivered via her brother along the lines of, 'Me and Ramos are going to Cannes to watch an awards ceremony. He can get you a ticket if you want to join us?' The birthday pool party had been the only one she'd accepted and that had been because Justin had asked her in front of their mum who, having recently completed her second round of chemotherapy, had been of the opinion that life was for living and insisted that she go. At that time, Flora would have jumped off a cliff if it had made her mum happy.

She'd been taken through the villa to the pool area and had caught her first glimpse of Ramos semi-naked since she'd seen him nude when she was thirteen. Her body had reacted in the exact same way it had then except this time there had been no bed for her to hide in.

She'd shrunk in on herself, feeling desperately out of place amongst all these rich, semi-naked, beautiful men and women who all knew each other well and were all laughing and drinking and throwing each other in the pool. Music had pounded out, competing with the screams of laughter, and she'd been so aware of the bikini-clad women flirting with Ramos. He'd been holding court like a king in his castle. It had made her sick to her stomach and she'd left his present, a hand-stitched embroidered portrait of his childhood dog she had spent hours making, on the table with all the other presents rather than approach him with it directly. She hadn't known what else to gift him. After all, what did you get the man who had everything?

He'd spotted her within minutes of her arrival, which was pretty impressive considering the huge size of the garden and the size of the posse surrounding him and considering that she'd been trying to blend in with one of the garden statues. His smile when he'd seen her... It had almost made her heart explode. He'd pointed at the changing rooms, indicating that was where she should get changed, but right then Flora had felt she would rather die than parade her body surrounded by all those perfectly formed glossy women.

She'd spent the next twenty minutes hiding in the changing rooms then feigned illness to Justin. Except it hadn't been fake. Her whole insides had cramped and for some stupid reason she'd been fighting back tears.

Ramos had followed her.

She hadn't expected that.

'You're not leaving already, are you?' he'd asked, eyes bright, teeth gleaming, tall, tanned, virile, half naked. 'You've come all this way.'

'I'm not feeling well,' she'd replied, avoiding his stare and walking quickly to the waiting cab to take her to her hotel. Justin had laughed when she'd booked the hotel, she remembered. Everyone would crash at Ramos's, he'd said. She thought now she'd already known how her evening would end.

Ramos had caught her hand. The smile had

left his face. 'If you're not well, you shouldn't be alone.'

'I'll be fine,' she'd muttered and yanked her burning hand out of his and thrown herself into the cab.

The next time she'd seen him had been at her mother's sick bed. He'd visited many times but she'd never allowed herself to be alone with him. The only reason she'd hung around during those visits was because she hadn't wanted to miss a minute of what was left of her mother's life.

He'd tried to engage Flora in conversation at the wake, she remembered. Asked how she was holding up. Asked if she was okay for money.

She'd barely been able to look him in the eye to politely tell him she was holding up fine and also fine for money.

'If you need anything, I'm always here,' he'd said.

Flora had bawled her eyes out during the funeral but that was the closest she'd come to tears at the wake. She'd had no idea why a touch of humanity from the man she despised had made her want to cry, but it had.

She'd managed to compress her lips into something that was supposed to resemble a smile and said, 'I've got Justin, but thank you,' before turning her back on him and going to sit with her grandfather.

The next time she'd seen him was the night they'd conceived their son, and she watched him lift Benjamin in the air again and place a kiss to his plump belly.

What was she holding out for? she wondered despondently. Night after night, sharing his bed, torturously aware and aroused.

She was scared. Admitting to herself that she'd essentially fancied Ramos since she was thirteen had been a huge thing, but to feel herself falling for him now, knowing that to give her body to him would be to give her heart…

If she could separate the physical from the emotional then she would be fine, but their one night together had proved she couldn't.

He'd crushed her heart the first time. Even if he hadn't misinterpreted her brother's message, he would have crushed her eventually, trading her in for the next pretty woman who caught his eye.

Ramos was a playboy. She believed he'd never cheated but he'd never been in a committed relationship before so how would he know how good his staying power was? How did he know what he'd do when his fleeting lust for her was spent and the next pretty thing came along?

And what if it never went that far? Her body had changed so much since their night together. What if it repulsed him? How could she bear it?

When Ramos crushed her heart again it would hurt much more than it had the first time because she was growing to like him. A lot.

If she wasn't careful, she would come to adore him.

Her heart did a sudden triple salchow when she noticed he was looking right back at her from the swimming pool.

He lifted a hand then took Benjamin's wrist and waved for him too.

She swallowed hard and waved back.

CHAPTER NINE

THAT NIGHT, EXCITEMENT and fear thrummed through Flora's veins as she dressed for the party they were going to hosted by an old friend of Ramos's. She hadn't dared ask if the friend had been at the pool party she'd run away from after thirty minutes. Or if any of the other guests had been there too. She doubted she would recognise them, not with their clothes on.

Ramos had said it wasn't a pool party, just a party-party and to dress accordingly, and she'd spent ages choosing an outfit from the beautiful array of couture clothes he'd insisted on buying her the other day. She could only hope she'd chosen a dress that wasn't going to make her feel like a frump in comparison to everyone else.

Not knowing which shoes to match with her outfit, a white, high-necked dress that landed below her knees and had the most fabulous floaty sleeves, she decided to bite the bullet, picked up two pairs and carried them through the main bedroom to his dressing room.

'Ramos?' she called from the archway.

He appeared and, for the longest time, did nothing but look her up and down.

'Do I look okay?' she asked anxiously, feeling even more insecure because he was dressed in a snazzy grey suit with an open-throated black shirt that only enhanced his fabulous physique.

'Querida...' His eyes glimmered. 'You look beautiful.'

Blushing, she held the shoes out. 'Which pair should I wear?'

His gaze drifted to her feet. She'd painted her toenails cherry red. 'I think you look damn sexy as you are.'

A flush coursed through her right from her painted toenails and rose up to the roots of her hair. 'I don't fancy getting cut feet,' she said, attempting lightness, 'so, please, which pair?'

His eyes swept from the shoes in her hands to her dress. 'Try the red pair first.'

Padding into his dressing room, she sat on the red velvet chaise longue and slipped her feet into the high red sandals, secured them, then stood up and held her arms out in a *'well?'*.

'Perfect,' he said.

She bit into her lip before blurting out, 'Does this dress make me look fat?'

Her question made his eyes narrow before dipping to her belly.

His chest rose, lips pulling together before he strode decisively to stand behind her, put his hands on her shoulders, and frogmarched her across the dressing room.

'What are you doing?' she asked.

'Making you look.'

'At what?'

He brought her to a stop in front of the walled mirror. 'At you.'

'I know what I look like.'

'Do you? Because that is not what your body language tells me. Please, *querida*, open your eyes and look.'

Sighing, trying her best to appear nonchalant that he was pressed lightly against her back, she raised her gaze to their reflection.

'There. I'm looking.' Looking at Ramos. The extra inches from the sandals had elevated her so she now reached his throat.

He rested his chin on the top of her head and, his reflected eyes glittering, moved his hands to hold her biceps.

'Do you know what I see?' he asked quietly.

She shook her head, suddenly unable to speak. There was an expression in his eyes that made her feel all choked.

'A beautiful woman. That's what I see,' he whispered. He ran his fingers through the ends of her hair loose around her shoulders. 'A woman with hair like silk.' He brushed his thumb at the small section of flesh exposed on her neck. She shivered at the sensation. 'A woman with skin like silk.'

His fingers tiptoed across her collarbone to reach the base of her throat. His hands flattened against the top of her chest. Slowly, he drew them down, over the swell of her breasts, and gently cupped them.

A tiny gasp flew from her mouth. Tiny because all the air had left her lungs.

His nose buried into her hair. His breath

swirled through the strands and penetrated her skull right through to her rapidly dizzying brain. 'A woman with breasts that are every bit as plump and beautiful now as they were the night we conceived our child.'

Flora tried to shake her head but the arousal flooding her overrode everything. All she could do was squeeze her eyes shut, grit her teeth, and fight desperately against the desire firing through every cell in her body.

His hands drifted to her belly, his mouth finding her ear. 'A woman with a stomach that carried and nurtured our child.'

The material of her dress swished around her knees, brushing against her increasingly fevered skin.

She needed to stop him…

Oh, God, he was gathering it together and pulling it up.

'Look, *querida.*'

Don't look. Whatever you do, don't look.

Her eyes flew back open.

The hooded sensuality in Ramos's reflected stare stole the last of her breath.

'Look,' he breathed.

One hand was flat against her pubis, the

other holding the material of her dress at the top of her hip, exposing her belly.

She barely registered her stomach, too intent on the gorgeous man gazing at her as if *she* were a thing of wonder.

'I see a woman,' he said hoarsely, his eyes taking her belly in before rising back up to gaze into her eyes. 'A sexy, beautiful, feminine, curvaceous woman who has given me the greatest gift a man can receive. Wear your curves with pride because you earned them and because they are as sexy as hell.'

Flora gazed, trapped and helpless, into Ramos's eyes. She needed to push his hand away and scream at him to stop but the heat bubbling inside her was too needy, too strong, melting her from the inside out.

His fingers slowly dipped under the band of her knickers.

Her knees buckled. Only his strength kept her upright.

She couldn't breathe. No matter how hard she tried, she couldn't draw in breath.

His fingers dipped lower.

Dear heavens, the sensation…

Her breath came back to her in shallow inhalations that turned into pants when a finger pressed gently against her swollen nub.

She was burning. Aflame.

He increased the pressure against her nub, just a little, but enough for...

Flora was losing herself. Losing control. Terrified, she struck out wildly behind her only for her hand to clasp tightly onto Ramos's hip, and then his mouth buried into her neck and she was lost.

Flopping her head back onto his shoulder, she closed her eyes and let herself go.

Moving her pelvis, she found a rhythm with the fingers doing such magical things to her. The pleasure was impossible to contain, escaping her lips in wanton moans as the pressure built up and up and she held on for dear life, writhing against him, suffused with his breath on her skin and in her hair and the whispers of his inaudible voice until, with a loud cry, the explosion came and shattered her into a million pieces.

'Flora?'

She didn't dare open her eyes.

Her dress had been released and gently

swooshed back to her knees. Two strong arms were wrapped around her waist holding her upright. Ramos's nose was nuzzling in her hair. He must be able to feel the thuds of her heart bashing through her.

She could still feel the zings of ecstasy that had split her body into mere atomic parts.

He whispered her name again.

But she couldn't respond. The second she opened her eyes or mouth, reality was going to hit her and then she would be confronted with the humiliation of how she had just come undone with nothing more than Ramos's touch.

He twisted her round to face him. Her legs obeyed his ministrations even if her brain tried to remain stubborn.

Warm hands cupped her cheeks.

'Flora, look at me,' he breathed.

She took a long breath, opened her eyes and met Ramos's melting stare.

She'd expected to find triumph there but what she found made her heart sigh and the potential for humiliation evaporate. There was no triumph, only wonder.

Incredibly, a tiny swell of laughter rose up

her throat. 'That wasn't supposed to happen,' she whispered, half smiling, half trying not to cry.

His lips curved and a low burst of laughter left his mouth before he lowered his face to hers and kissed her. It was the lightest brush of his lips against hers but, oh, thank the Lord he was holding her up or she would have swooned to the floor.

His hands skimmed from her cheeks to thread through the strands of her hair.

And then he kissed her again, harder, with a greedy possessiveness that knitted all her atoms back together and pulsed them back to glorious life.

This time Flora accepted the loss of control and melted into the heady heat of his hungry mouth.

A loud noise cut right through them and, eyes locking back together, both pulled their faces away so only the tips of their noses touched. Ramos's ragged breath was warm against her sensitised lips, and her mouth tingled for more of his kisses, her skin burning for more of his touch...

More of everything.

The loud tune continued its incessant hum until Ramos stepped back and pulled his phone out of his pocket. He swiped it without even looking at the screen and threw it onto the sofa.

His chest rising and falling in great heaves, he held his hand out to her.

Feeling as if she were in the midst of a dream, Flora threaded her fingers into his and let him lead her into the bedroom. There, he pushed her gently on the bed.

He stared at her for the longest time and for a moment she was taken back to the look in his eyes the moment before their lips had brushed together for the very first time.

That was the night she had gone to him pleading for his mercy.

She'd looked in those spellbinding dark eyes and had run out of words. She'd lost the power of speech. In that moment, the only thought in her head had been that Alejandro Ramos was beautiful.

Alone as they had never been alone before, there had been no one to distract her, no one to rescue her.

She hadn't needed rescuing from Ramos. She'd needed rescuing from herself.

Trapped in the swirling depths, her heart a sharp, painful tattoo, she'd been overcome with the need to feel *his* heart and had placed her hand on his chest before she was aware of what she was doing. He'd sucked in a breath at her touch, she remembered. The hard beats had thumped against her palm. Spellbound, she'd cupped his cheek. He'd been unshaven. The look she could see in his eyes now had rung out starkly when he'd whispered her name. Slowly, his mouth had inched closer and at that very first brush of his lips to hers, she'd been lost.

And now she was caught again and she no longer had the strength or the will to fight it.

She no longer *wanted* to fight it.

Ramos shrugged his jacket off and let it drop on the floor. Eyes not leaving her face, he undid the buttons of his shirt and let that drop too.

Flora, her heart beating fast, unashamedly drank him in.

Hadn't she known since that adolescent glimpse of his nudity that Alejandro Ramos was the epitome of masculine perfection, the physical standard for which she put all men but which no other could live up to?

He wore his rampant sexuality like a cloak, his melting eyes hypnotising and luring. Hadn't that been why she'd always avoided looking in his eyes? Hadn't she instinctively known as a young adolescent the danger that lay for her in those depths, known that they were a trap, just as she'd know his very scent was a trap to entice her too?

His hands went to his chinos.

His erection was clearly delineated beneath the fabric.

The pulse between her legs throbbed.

God, she wanted him. Desperately. A wanton craving that existed only for him.

She put a hand to the bulge in his chinos and traced the hard length.

His strong throat swallowed.

Tilting her head back to gaze up at his gorgeous face and to revel in the desire blazing from it, she undid the button of his trousers.

Working quickly, jaw clenched, he removed the rest of his clothes.

His erection sprang free, as huge and glorious as she remembered, and the pulse between her legs throbbed even deeper.

He stepped to her and put his hands to her thighs. And then he parted them. Kneeling on the floor before her, he slid his hands under the skirt of her dress and up, over her hips to catch the band of her knickers in his fingers.

The beats of her heart now smashing against her ribs, her breaths coming in quick bursts, Flora lifted her bottom to help him tug them down. Knickers removed, he unbuckled her sandals and threw them behind him with the other discarded clothes...and then he kissed a cherry-red painted toenail. And then his lips pressed over the arch of her foot to her ankle, brushing up her calf and over her knee, the marks of his mouth and tongue leaving a scorching trail of lightning in their wake, up the highly sensitised flesh of her thighs, hands gripping her dress and pushing it up, exposing her pubis...

She flopped onto her back with a gasp when his tongue found the sweet spot his fingers had so recently brought to a peak.

Alejandro had a magical power over her,

she thought dreamily as she willingly submitted to the unrelenting pleasure. He could melt her insides with nothing but a look and turn her into a mass of nerves and sensations with only the lightest of touches. His magic was stronger than her defences and when it felt this good, this essential, she could think of no good reason to fight it any more, not when surrender felt so incredible.

The sensations building deep inside her were coiling together, swelling and thickening but, just as stars were starting to form behind her eyes, he moved his mouth from her heart and up, over her belly, pushing her dress as far as it would rise.

Feeling drugged on lust, craving the feel of his skin pressed tightly against hers, Flora undid the clasp at the neck of her dress. Working together, they pulled it off before he deftly unclasped her bra and replaced the lace with his mouth. With sounds of greedy appreciation, he sucked and licked, traced his tongue around the peaks, making her head flop back again at the intoxicating pleasure of it.

It was *all* pleasure. The magic of his mouth.

The magic of his hands exploring the contours of her body. The magic of his smooth skin beneath her own exploring hands. The softness of his hair and the hardness of his body. The musk of his skin and the spiciness of his cologne. It all infused her senses and fed her increasing desperation for his possession, and when he snaked his tongue up her neck and pinned his elbows either side of her face to gaze down at her, Flora saw the passion burning her matched in his liquid stare.

His hooded eyes were eating her alive.

Suddenly desperate to be as one with him, Flora clasped the back of his head and lifted her head to fuse her mouth to his.

He groaned, and kissed her back so ravenously she could taste his hunger for her. Tongues clashing and dancing, she wound her legs around his waist and arched upwards at the same moment he thrust himself deep inside her.

The sensation was so incredible that stars flashed behind her eyes.

There was a long moment of stillness before he raised his head. Breathing deeply, he gazed into her eyes. The emotion pouring from his stare penetrated her as deeply as he was buried in her.

Please, let it feel as magical for him as it does for me, she prayed. *Let Alejandro feel all of this as deeply and as profoundly as I do.*

He kissed her.

She wound her arms tightly around him and closed her eyes.

Breasts crushed against chest, they drove the pleasure higher. In and out he thrust, each movement taking her closer to saturation point, closer still, until he clasped her bottom, fusing their groins together, and she shot past every peak he'd taken her to before and, with spasms of pleasure exploding through her, she soared high into the sky, over kaleidoscopic stars, his name falling from her tongue, her own name shooting from his lips a distant echo caressing her ears.

Slowly, so slowly, Flora floated down from the stars.

Alejandro was slumped on top of her, breathing heavily into her neck. The thuds of his heart beat through her skin to her own cantering heart.

Alejandro was the star, she realised as she landed like a feather back on the earth rotating around him. She was the earth unable to escape his gravitational pull.

Was she in love with him? Or was it just lust?

The answer made her heart clench.

She'd been in some form of love with Alejandro Ramos for half her life. It had been a form of sickness, a violent tempest of emotions she'd been far too young to handle or understand. It had stopped her ever looking at other men. Until the night they'd conceived their child, her only kiss from a boy had come from a game of kiss chase in primary school.

She thought back to their first night together. He'd made love to her with a tenderness that had filled her chest with so many emotions it had turned her into putty in his hands.

She'd wished many times that he'd been a selfish oaf of a lover because then it might have made the pain that had lanced her when he'd stood her up the next night and then cut her so effectively out of his life easier to bear.

An icy sliver of panic washed through her now. What if this had all been an elaborate hoax to reel her back in one more time before he discarded her again?

'Say something,' he whispered, raising his head and lifting much of his weight off her.

Afraid to look in his eyes, more afraid not to, Flora plucked up the courage to gaze into the swirling depths. Whatever the emotion she was looking at was, it melted the icy panic.

Because there was emotion there. She could see it. Deep emotion.

But hadn't she seen it that night too? Wasn't that why his cruel treatment of her had cut so deeply?

Things had been different then, she reminded herself. Very different. They had a child now. They were married. He wore a ring on his finger that told the world he belonged to her.

'Say something,' he repeated. 'Please. Tell me what you're thinking.'

Exhaling a slow breath, she smiled. 'Who was on the phone?'

His brow furrowed and then his mouth widened into the heartbreaking smile she'd always hated because of what it did to her heart, and he chuckled lightly and kissed her.

'I've no idea who called me. Now, tell me what you're really thinking,' he insisted, smoothing his thumbs over her forehead.

He was still inside her.

'We didn't use protection?' she suggested as an alternative to the truth.

His eyebrows rose and then he chuckled again. 'See what you do to me, *querida*. You make me lose my mind.'

'Good,' she whispered, the feigned nonchalance deserting her. 'Because you make me lose my mind too.' He made her lose her mind, her inhibitions and all her sensibilities. Barely an hour ago she would have freaked out at the very thought of having unprotected sex with Alejandro.

And that was what he did to her and why she'd fought her desire for so long. One burst of uncontrolled passion and already she was imagining the beautiful baby they might

have created through it. He made her want…
no, crave…so much. All with him.

He kissed her again, more deeply. More
possessively.

She wanted to cry when he broke the kiss
and then broke the other connection between
them to roll onto his back.

Turning his face to her, he took her hand
and brought it to his lips. She rolled onto
her side facing him and threaded her fingers
through his.

'How would you feel if we have made another baby?' he asked, his expression serious.

Wondering if he could read her mind, she
nudged her face closer to his. 'Not unhappy.'
She was quite sure she should be unhappy
about it but in this post-coital haze—and she
was glad she had enough wits about her to
know it *was* a post-coital haze—the thought
of having another baby, and this time going
through the whole pregnancy with Alejandro
at her side, made her heart feel as if it could
burst. 'What about you?'

His lips quirked. 'Not unhappy.'

'You want more babies?'

'Sure. You?'

'Until about a minute ago, I hadn't really thought about it.'

'I have.'

She hesitated before asking, 'With me?'

He kissed the tips of her fingers, his gaze not wavering. 'Only you.'

Her heart swelled so much she really thought it had burst.

'You're serious?' she whispered.

'Flora…' He sighed and closed his eyes. When he opened them back onto her, he let go of her hand and twisted onto his side. Pulling her flush against him, he stroked her hair and said, 'You are my wife. Whatever the reasons for why we married, I chose to marry you.'

'Because you didn't want me to keep Benjamin from you or poison him against you,' she reminded him.

His smile was rueful. 'I don't think I believed even then that you would do that.'

'You didn't?'

'No woman who could devote such time and love to her sick mother would treat her child like a weapon.'

Hot tears welled and stabbed the backs of her eyes, but she didn't know where they came from. The tenderness in his voice? The memory of those dark days when Flora wouldn't leave her mum's side? She hadn't wanted strangers, no matter how compassionate and lovely they were, doing her mother's intimate care.

Swallowing back the tears, she said, 'So why did you marry me if you knew I wouldn't keep Benjamin from you?'

He stared silently at her for so long that she wondered if he was trying to read her innermost thoughts, but then he shook his head and grimaced. 'It is done. We are here, we are married and we have a son. If you are happy to have more children, then that is great. I don't want Benjamin to be on his own like I was.'

Now she was the one to stare into his eyes and try to read his mind but her mind-reading skills were poor, and she didn't want to ruin the moment by forcing a confession of something that would probably hurt her. Back then, he'd hated her. What else was there to know?

She saw no hate in his eyes now. 'Do you believe me now?' she whispered. 'About our night together?'

His mouth formed a tight line before loosening. Closing his eyes, he pressed his forehead lightly to hers and kissed the tip of her nose. 'Yes, *querida*. I believe you.'

The relief at this was overwhelming and, for the second time in as many minutes, she had to swallow back tears.

Flora hadn't realised how much it had eaten at her that Alejandro had convinced himself that she'd only slept with him for her brother's freedom.

When she was certain she'd contained the emotion bubbling inside her, she softly said, 'What you said about not wanting Benjamin to be on his own like you were...did you want a sibling?'

'Yes.'

'Were you a lonely child?'

'Sometimes. Because my father travelled so much with his work and we travelled everywhere with him, I didn't go to school until I was ten.'

'That was because of your mother's death,

wasn't it?' she asked, and had to swallow back another swell of emotion.

Was this what it was like for all women after sex? Did it send their emotions all over the place too? Or was it just the effect Alejandro had on her?

He nodded. 'I had nannies and an English tutor until then.'

'That must have been a hard adjustment to make. Going to school, I mean.'

His face creased with surprise. 'Not at all. I was glad to go. It is hard for a child to make friends when they are never in the same place for longer than a week.'

'But if you'd never been to school before, that would have been a brand-new environment for you. That would have frightened the hell out of me at ten.'

His voice was steady but she thought she heard an edge to it. 'I watched my mother's coffin be buried in the ground two weeks before I started school. I told you before, nothing has frightened or hurt me since and nothing ever will.'

She stared at his face, noting the underlying hardness that had just formed in his expression. It was similar to the hardness she saw whenever her brother's name was mentioned.

Palming the side of his neck, she brushed her thumb over his smooth skin and wished she could dive into his heart and smooth out the suffering he'd lived through.

For the first time she understood him. Truly understood him.

Alejandro had lived through a child's worst nightmare and survived it, but it had damaged a core part of him. He was like those deep-sea squids she'd read about who, when feeling threatened, attacked the predator and then pulled away breaking off the tip of their own arm. Except, in Alejandro's case, it wasn't predators he attacked, it was people who hurt him, his attack a defence mechanism crucial to his survival.

He'd ruthlessly severed Justin from his life without seeking or wanting an explanation for his out-of-character behaviour, just turned his back on thirteen years of close friendship and gone full steam ahead on the attack. Whatever Alejandro said to the contrary, Flora was certain that on some fundamental level Justin's theft—more likely the situation that had led up to it—had hurt him.

What had the cost of severing his closest friend been to himself?

He'd cut Flora from his life too. Made love to her with such tenderness and then, believing she'd used him, deliberately and remorselessly dropped her from a great height.

She'd heard other stories of his hard-heartedness too, like the one of the good friend for whom Alejandro had been best man at his wedding, who had been suspected of tipping off the press about minor stories of him and cut from his circle and discarded without afterthought for it.

When Ramos cut someone from his life, there was no way back. Flora was the only exception to this severing and that was only because of Benjamin.

When emotionally threatened, he was ruthless. And remorseless. She must never forget that.

The hardness in his stare softened. 'You are beautiful, did you know that?'

She tried to smile.

He inched his face closer to hers. 'Very

beautiful. I remember seeing you at your twenty-first birthday…' He brushed his lips to hers. 'Hillier's annoying little sister all grown up.' He kissed her again. 'You took my breath away.'

'I did?'

'You still do.' Tongue sweeping into her mouth, he rolled back on top of her and sent her back to the stars.

CHAPTER TEN

Two and a half hours after they were supposed to set off for the party, they got in the back of the car. Alejandro was unperturbed about their tardiness, pointing out that most parties took a few hours to warm up and that no party really got going until he arrived. The latter was a point she was not going to argue with. She couldn't really argue about the former either. Flora had never been a party animal, not even close, had always preferred nights out with her small group of close friends to raucous shindigs.

Now wearing a black wrap dress—when they'd finally dragged themselves out of bed she'd found the white one scrunched on the floor—and with her hair now tied into a loose bun, Flora resisted attaching herself to him like a limpet and satisfied her body's craving for him by holding his hand.

The post-coital bliss of their second lovemaking still thrummed in her veins but the barriers she'd worn around him for so many years were refortifying themselves.

She no longer denied that she was in love with him but she wasn't so far gone that she couldn't protect the last part of her heart from him. So long as she kept a degree of detachment, she could survive marriage to a man who could never love her.

Love involved risk. It involved hurt. Alejandro would never allow himself to love anyone because the risk of hurt was too strong a deterrent for him.

He had feelings for her. Strong feelings, she was certain.

But they weren't strong enough for him to take the risk of love and if he ever found out how deeply her feelings for him ran, the tipping point of power in their marriage would fall even more heavily in his favour.

The party was in a traditional Spanish villa that matched Alejandro's for size and elegance, their hosts a wildly glamorous couple called Juan and Camila who greeted Flora with enormous kisses to her cheek and a large glass of champagne.

Having only had that tiny glass of wine over dinner the night of the ballet since Benjamin's conception, Flora knew she needed to take it easy with the alcohol. The problem was, Alejandro had been righter than even she had suspected that the party wouldn't start until he arrived, and no sooner had they entered the vast party room than all the beautiful, glamourous guests clamoured around him. Although most spoke in Spanish, she could tell by their tone and body language that they were chiding him, and guessed it was because he'd been off the party scene for so long. With everyone wanting a piece of the only person she knew there, and feeling the weight of a hundred pairs of curious eyes and so many introductions made and kisses planted on her cheeks, Flora kept sipping at her champagne out of nerves and before she knew it, she'd finished two full glasses.

'Let me show you our new swimming pool,' her hostess insisted, taking the empty glass from her and handing it to a passing waiter. Camila then slipped her arm through Flora's and bore her away.

Flora looked over her shoulder at Alejandro and her stomach settled a little when she immediately caught his eye and received a faint, knowing wink from him.

The far end of the party room had no wall and led straight onto the terrace, which acted like an extension of the party room and was filled with numerous people enjoying the humidity of the hot evening. After the air conditioning of the villa's interior, Flora felt the heat, and when Camila snatched another glass of champagne for her, she took a large mouthful of it without even realising.

'You are Justin's sister?' Camila said as they walked down marble steps to the large kidney-shaped swimming pool.

'Yes.'

'I remember you.'

Her heart sank. 'Do you?'

'A party at Alejandro's a few years ago.'

'You have a good memory.'

'You were the only one wearing clothes,' Camila pointed out with a cackle of laughter that made Flora grin. 'My sister was hoping

Alejandro would notice her but he only had eyes for you.'

'Hardly,' she demurred, feeling a blush crawl over her face. 'I was only there for thirty minutes.' And most of that had been spent hiding in the changing room.

'He didn't want her after you went.' Camila nudged Flora's side with her elbow. 'That was very unusual. It is why I was not surprised when I heard he had married you, even though you are Justin's sister.'

She didn't have the faintest idea how to take that or how she should respond.

They reached the water's edge.

'I miss your brother,' Camila said. 'We were lovers many years ago.'

'Maybe a bit too much information?' Flora suggested. 'I am his sister.'

'It is okay, I will not give you details of his lovemaking. How is he?'

'Lonely. Guilty. Ashamed.'

Camila gave a nonchalant shrug. 'He should be ashamed. He screwed his best friend.'

'I know.' Justin would live with the guilt and regret for the rest of his life.

She sighed. 'But I still miss him. I bet Alejandro does too.'

Flora would bet on it too.

'And it is good that he is here tonight. We have all missed him.'

'Sorry.' She had no idea why she was apologising. 'We've been a bit busy with Benjamin.'

'It has been much longer than that since he stopped seeing his friends.'

'What do you mean?'

'A year? Longer, I think. A little after we learned Justin had stolen all that money from him.'

Around the time of Benjamin's conception, then?

Coincidence?

'What are you two gossiping about?' a deep voice asked from behind them.

'You, of course,' Camila answered with a cackle while Flora hastily downed the rest of her champagne.

Alejandro noticed and raised an eyebrow.

Flora shrugged in a 'no, I don't know why I did that' manner.

He smirked before turning his attention to

Camila. 'I hope you haven't been telling my wife too many horror stories about me.'

'I haven't had the time, so if you could leave us alone a bit longer...'

'No.'

'It's okay,' Flora piped up. 'I've already heard most of them.'

Camila cackled even louder, and said something to Alejandro in Spanish before heading back, still laughing, to the other revellers.

'What did she say?' Flora asked.

'That she likes you.'

'Really?'

'Yes.' He wrapped his arms around her and pulled her flush to him. 'Tell me the horror stories you have heard about me.'

'I didn't hear *about* them. I *heard* them.'

'What do you mean?'

'When you used to stay at our house, you and Justin would often go out for the night.' Whenever Justin brought Ramos home for a weekend they would be inundated with party invitations from Justin's old school friends. 'I would listen out for you to get home and then sneak out of my bedroom and sit at the top of the stairs listening to you discuss how the night had gone.'

He winced. 'Really?' he asked doubtfully.

She hooked her arms around his neck. 'Sometimes when I was feeling *really* brave, I would sneak down the stairs and hide behind doors.'

'Even when you were young?'

'I was thirteen when I started eavesdropping on you.'

A faint look of alarm flickered over his face. 'So I would have been twenty?'

'Yep.' She raised herself onto her toes and grazed her teeth over his chin. 'You were a bad boy.'

'You shouldn't have been listening, not at that age.' He shook his head. 'I didn't know.'

'I was very quiet.' She dropped her voice to a whisper. 'Like a little stealthy mouse.'

His eyes narrowed but there was amusement in them. 'How much have you had to drink?'

'Three glasses of champagne. Why? Am I drunk?'

'Do you feel drunk?'

'I don't know. I've never been drunk before.'

'Never?'

'Uh-uh.'

'Why not?'

'I didn't want to be one of those women.'

'What women?'

'You know. *Those* women. The kind who threw themselves at you.'

'Did you think you would be like them if you had a drink?'

'Alcohol makes you love…lose…your inhi…' She hiccuped. 'Inhibitions!' she finished triumphantly.

'Did you think you would throw yourself at me?'

'Not saying.'

'Why not?'

'You'll get a big head.'

'What were you scared of?'

'Falling in love with you, silly.'

Her eyesight had become a bit blurry but she thought she saw the amusement fall from his face. Her sight wasn't quite clear enough to see what replaced it.

'Come on,' he said, brushing a gentle kiss to her lips, 'let's get you home.'

'But we've only just got here. I'm having a lovely time.'

'There will be other parties.'

'Promise?'

'Promise.'

'Alejandro?'

He sucked in a breath. 'Yes, *querida*?'

'I don't feel very well.'

Someone had inserted a hammer into Flora's head and was merrily smashing it into her skull.

She opened an eye. The room was dusky.

There was movement beside her and then Alejandro sat on the bed. He was fully dressed.

He touched her forehead. 'You okay?' he murmured.

'No.'

He grinned. 'There is water and painkillers on the bedside table.'

'Thank you,' she whispered. 'What time is it?'

'Eight.'

She tried to lift her head, but, ow!

He chuckled.

The noise made her wince. 'Don't,' she moaned.

'Sorry,' he said in a completely unapologetic tone.

'Where's Benjamin?'

'With Sinead.'

'I should get up.'

'You should sleep more,' he said firmly. 'Water and sleep are the best cures for hangovers.'

'Thank you for looking after me.' She had vague memories of him helping her to the car, helping her into it, helping her crawl out of it, helping her navigate the stairs to their room, then helping her undress.

'De nada.'

She bit her lip as another vague memory filtered through her heavy head of trying to get him to make love to her and him kissing her forehead and telling her to go to sleep.

'Did I embarrass you?'

The grin returned. 'No.

She sighed. 'I'm sorry.'

He leaned over and kissed her. 'Don't be.'

Then he grinned again. 'Twenty-four and suffering your first hangover.'

'And my last.'

Still grinning, he gave her another kiss. 'I have to go.'

Her mood went from hungover but happy to hungover and miserable in an instant.

'Now?' she asked, trying not to sound too forlorn about it.

This was his first business trip since his early return from Las Vegas.

'I have meetings in Athens at midday.'

But it's Sunday, she wanted to howl.

Hotel casinos didn't have the same working days as normal businesses.

'I'll be back Saturday. Friday if I can.'

'Call me when you get there so I know you've arrived safely?'

He stared at her with the strangest expression on his face before bowing his head. 'Of course.'

Flora concentrated very hard on not crying when he closed the door softly behind him.

The days without Alejandro dragged by.

Flora had thought herself accustomed to

him being away so much but, having had him to herself for a week and with the closeness and intimacy that had developed between them in that time, she felt his absence in Athens starkly.

If not for Benjamin, she feared she would have cracked and begged him on one of their evening calls—he now called every night—to let her fly out to him, which would have been the worst thing she could have done and just reeked of desperation and exposed herself to him far more than their lovemaking had done.

But she did have her bundle of joy and it was impossible to mope with Benjamin's happy little smiling face loving her and needing her. Other than Hangover Sunday, when Flora finally managed to drag herself out of bed at ten a.m., poor Sinead hadn't had much to do apart from flirt with Mateo.

Flora also thought she had found a friend in Camila. The glamourous Spanish lady invited herself over for lunch and turned up with her toddler, an adorable little girl called Ava whose curly golden hair Benjamin kept trying to grab. He seemed smitten.

Camila was great fun and wildly indiscreet, and when she left, she extracted a promise from Flora to join her and some other 'girls' on a night out soon.

It was the evenings she most missed Alejandro. Benjamin filled her days but he was always asleep by seven, which left hours to fill before she could find sleep of her own. She bought some embroidery supplies but inspiration and creativity had still deserted her. She tried to read a book but her attention span was decimated.

Thursday evening, the same day Camila had come for lunch, she gave up trying to do anything that involved concentration and, after putting Sinead in charge should Benjamin wake up, headed to the roof terrace.

The roof terrace was something she'd only had a curious look at before. Enclosed by a waist-height white wall, it had a seating area and a dining area and a fully stocked bar, but it was the L-shaped swimming pool she'd come up here for.

Making sure her phone's volume was high, so she'd hear it when Alejandro called, she placed it on her towel then lowered herself into the underlit water. It felt deliciously cool in contrast to the humid heat of the evening, and she kept her head above water and swam a couple of lengths of the longest part, then hugged the edge as she trod water and gazed out at the spectacular view of Barcelona by night. The city's skyscape, somehow surrounding her but feeling as if it was far away too, was a golden silhouette. Shining above it all this moonless night were so many stars it made her feel dizzy to imagine their numbers.

It made her feel dizzy, too, to remember how her mouth had run away with her at Camila and Juan's party. She'd forgotten all about it until long after Alejandro had flown to Athens and her cheeks had gone so red she could have used them as handwarmers.

Her refusal to partake in more than a small glass of wine before that night had been down to Alejandro. And her brother. Eavesdropping on their drunk talk about conquests and the wild things the girls at parties had done had been a more effective alcohol deterrent than any lecture by an adult. Until Saturday, she'd never been drunk. The thought of being picked apart and rated had revolted her.

So why had she listened in; hidden behind doors like a miniature spy, hardly daring to breathe for fear of being discovered? More than once Alejandro had strolled past her hiding space without noticing her.

Camila's indiscretions that day had been mostly about Justin. Alejandro had been mentioned too but she'd had a feeling Camila had made a conscious effort not to speak of his dalliances with other women to her. Justin had been the focus of her talk, making Flora wonder if she still hankered after him.

All Camila's indiscretions had made Flora rethink the drunk conversations she'd avidly eavesdropped on.

Justin had been the one to do all the rating, she remembered. Alejandro had laughed along with it, but Justin had always been the instigator of those conversations.

He'd been trying to impress him, she realised.

And she realised too that it had been easier on her heart to blame his behaviour on his Spanish friend rather than confront the brother who'd always adored and looked out for her for being a sexist pig.

Alejandro had been wild too but he'd never boasted about it. He'd never strung women along or messed them around or made promises he wouldn't keep. She supposed he'd never needed to.

Or maybe he was just a damn sight more respectful than she'd given him credit for.

She'd childishly hated him for stealing Justin from her and then she'd seen him naked and hated him even more for the terrifying feelings his nakedness had awoken in her.

He'd deserved none of her misplaced hate. He'd been a red-blooded young man playing the field, partying and enjoying his life. He couldn't help that he was drop-dead gorgeous, filthy rich, and that women salivated over him.

She rested her chin on her hands with a sad sigh.

She missed him. That was the truth. Even when the only emotion she'd dared allow herself to admit to feeling for him had been loathing, his presence had always energised her. The world always felt a little flatter without him in it.

It felt a lot flatter now.

'There you are.'

A short scream of fright escaped her throat before the joy of recognition thrashed through her and she twisted round to see Alejandro silhouetted on the poolside.

CHAPTER ELEVEN

IT DIDN'T EVEN cross Flora's mind to play it cool. She couldn't have stopped the beaming smile from forming even if she'd tried. 'You're back!'

Pushing her feet off the pool's side to propel her, she swam over to him. The water's depth there came to her breasts and she put her feet on the bottom and her hands on the edge of the pool, and gazed up at his gorgeous face. 'You've grown a beard.'

He stroked it. 'You like?'

'It's okay.' She grinned. It was more than okay. It made him look even sexier, something she would never have thought possible. 'How come you're back?'

He leaned over and removed his shoes and socks. 'I cancelled the rest of my meetings.'

She drank him in. 'Why?'

He straightened, fingers on a shirt button, his eyes capturing hers. 'I missed my family.'

Her heart swelled. 'You should have told me you were coming home.'

'I wanted it to be a surprise... Is it?'

'Well, duh.'

'I mean, is it a good surprise?'

'It's okay.' Her mouth forming another beaming smile totally negated her efforts at nonchalance.

His teeth flashed, eyes crinkling. His shirt went flying behind him. 'You have missed me?'

Desperately. 'It's...different when you're not here.'

His naked chest rose and his glimmering gaze stayed on her even as he undid his trousers. 'I missed you.'

Her heart swelled so much at this admission that it stuck in her throat.

Now fully naked, his discarded clothes scattered all around him, Alejandro dropped himself into the water next to her and put his hands on her hips, twisting her round to face him.

'*Did* you miss me?' he asked, sliding his arms around her back to hold her closer.

Winding her arms around his neck, she

tilted her head back and sighed her pleasure at being back in his arms, then raised herself up on the tips of her toes to kiss him.

He moved his head back before her lips could connect and fixed a stern stare on her. 'Did you miss me?'

Flora stared into the dark, melting eyes she had missed more than she'd believed was humanly possible but something held her back from making that confession.

Alejandro had so much power over her. More power than he knew. Emotional power.

He was Flora's one and only. Her feelings for him ran so deep they were an intrinsic part of her, but for her to admit any part of it would be to hand him even more power. To admit to any part of it would be to put it out in the open. Would make it real.

Words that were said could never be unsaid.

The sternness dissolved, replaced by a knowing gleam, and he clasped his hands to her waist and lifted her high off her feet.

Instinctively, she wrapped her legs around his waist and was rewarded with the hard tip of his erection jutting against the fold of her sex. Only the material of her swimsuit stopped him diving straight into her.

He carried her up the gentle slope of the pool's floor until he found the perfect height to sit her on the pool's edge, groin to groin.

Only then did he kiss her, and, dear heaven, what a kiss it was, a slow fusion of lips and the slow stroke of his tongue against hers, as seductive, sensual and perfect a kiss as it was possible to have.

When he broke it, she whimpered at the loss of the pleasure.

He gazed back into her eyes and growled before spearing her hair to clasp her head and devour her mouth again.

Flora tightened her hold around his neck and revelled in the taste of his mouth and all the heady sensations fizzing and bubbling through her veins, her skin, every component of her. And then he danced his lips across her cheek to lick the lobe of her ear and bury his face into her neck. His beard scratched deliciously against her sensitised skin and she moaned, digging her nails into his skull until he put a hand to her chest and gently but firmly pushed her back so he had better access to assault her with his mouth while tugging her swimsuit off her shoulders.

Impatient to be as naked as him, she pulled her arms free and pulled her swimsuit down to her waist.

'Did you miss me?' he asked.

'Just kiss me,' she said, throwing her arms back around his neck and crushing her mouth to his, pressing every inch of her that she could to him.

Alejandro was much stronger than her and easily slipped a hand between their conjoined chests to gently push her back again.

Eyes ablaze with sensuality, he gripped hold of her swimsuit with one hand, raised her bottom with the other, and stepped back to pull it down to her thighs. In seconds she'd kicked it off and hooked her ankles behind his muscular butt to reel him back to her.

He growled again and dipped his head to take a breast into his mouth.

Heavens, that felt so...

Flora closed her eyes and let the sensations infuse her, crying out when he cupped her other breast and kneaded it with just the right amount of pressure, straddling the line between pleasure and pain but never letting it spill over to anything that wasn't bliss.

His touch set her on fire.

He set her on fire. Stopped her seeing straight or thinking clearly. Turned her into a mass of nerves that cried out for him.

'Did you miss me?' he asked again, dragging his fingers down over her belly. She would have blocked out the question, but there was something about the hoarseness in his voice that made her open her eyes. What she saw in the tautness of his face had her slide her hands over his chest, skimming her fingers through the fine dark hair to rest them at his throat.

He must have drugged her with his kisses and his touch because she stared into his eyes and whispered, 'Yes.'

His chest and shoulders rose slowly and heavily and then he kissed her with such hunger that any fear of handing him the power of her feelings was consumed in the headiness of his passion, and she was consumed too, with the need to taste and touch him.

Trailing her fingers down his muscular

arms, she ran her tongue down the column of his throat, bringing her hands onto his chest, flattening them, dragging them down his hard abdomen as she lowered her head to take a flat, brown nipple into her mouth.

He groaned and fisted her hair. His erection was jutting into her thigh, just out of reach of where she most wanted it, and, biting gently onto his other nipple, she dipped her hand further down, through the coarser dark pubic hair, and took hold of it.

His grip on her hair tightened.

She looked up, into his eyes. 'Show me how,' she whispered.

'Flora...'

She bit his nipple again, felt the shudder that rippled through him, and looked back up at him. 'Show me,' she commanded with all the sensuality she possessed.

He swallowed, then his much bigger hand covered hers.

Glazed eyes locked on hers, he adjusted her hold around it then slowly began to move her hand, first down his rock-hard length to the base, and then back up to the head, down then up… And then he released her hand and closed his eyes as she continued the movements exactly as he'd shown her. When she gripped it a little tighter, his mouth opened but the only sound to come out was dim, shallow breaths.

'Am I doing it right?' she whispered huskily.

His eyes opened.

He snatched her hand away from him and held it tightly at her side as he brought his face to hers.

For the longest moment he did nothing but gaze at her, gaze so intensely it was as if he were peering down into her soul.

'You are beautiful,' he growled.

And then Alejandro plunged into her and Flora fell into the melting swirl of his eyes.

It was too late for rescue, she thought dimly as she drowned in the intensity of his lovemaking.

She loved him. Loved him, loved him. With her heart, her body and soul.

She held him tight, infusing herself with his scent and the taste of his skin. The pleasure he was giving her filled her completely, soaked into every hidden part, then, as his thrusts deepened and his mouth captured hers, their eyes locked back together and she flew over the edge. Spasms pulsated in waves through her, and she let them carry her over the mountainous crests, staring at Alejandro's face as it tightened then contorted and a roar was buried into her neck as his release came in wild, convulsive bucks.

Flora tried not to flinch or laugh. She tried really hard. Really, really hard.

Her thighs flinched at the same moment she grabbed hold of her pillow and giggled into it.

The bedsheets around her waist flew back and Alejandro's stern face appeared from between her legs. 'Why are you laughing?'

'You're tickling me.'

'You said you weren't ticklish.'

'How was I supposed to know my thighs are ticklish? No one's ever tickled them with a feather before.'

Smugness replaced the sternness.

'What's that look for?' she asked, suspicious.

His stare was lascivious. 'I like knowing there has been only me for you.'

She scowled and threw her pillow at him.

'Hey, what was that for?' He chucked the pillow on the floor and crawled up to hover over her.

'When you say things like that it reminds me that I'm not the only one for you.'

'Do you see anyone else in this bed?' he deadpanned.

'Ha, ha.'

'You are jealous of my past?'

'Don't be ridiculous,' she lied primly. 'It's just not...very gentlemanly to remind me of it.'

He stroked her hair from her forehead and smiled. 'I like it when you're jealous.'

'I'm not jealous, but why do you like it?'

'It shows you feel something for me.'

'I do feel something for you, Ramos. Lust.'

Now he was the one to scowl. 'When will you call me Alejandro?'

She shrugged. 'Our tenth wedding anniversary?'

'Ha-ha,' he mimicked. Then he grinned again. 'And you feel more for me than lust. You miss me when I'm away, just as I miss you.'

'I miss your lovemaking.' There. She could admit that to him.

Truth was, she needed their breaks from each other to recover herself. The urge to tell him she loved him and confess every hidden depth of her feelings for him often came close to overwhelming her.

The times he spent away from them had decreased dramatically since they had become lovers two months ago. Now he was only away a couple of nights a week, three at the most. He said it was because he couldn't bear being parted from his family any longer than that, and she couldn't do anything to stop the leap of hope that he meant her as well as Benjamin.

He told her he missed her but never had he suggested she join him on his work travels. So she didn't suggest it either. She didn't believe he was seeing other women though, not when he was always so hungry for her.

To think she'd worried he would find her body repulsive!

It wasn't just in the bedroom that he showed he cared. He liked to surprise her with trips away. There had been a long weekend in Ibiza with a meal at a restaurant that was like no restaurant she'd ever been to; a futuristic sensory experience that had blown her mind. A weekend shopping in New York. A trip for her birthday to Niagara Falls. A week sailing the Caribbean. And so much more besides, all with Benjamin and the nanny in tow, a family unit.

But for all that, never did he ask her to accompany him on his business trips.

'Is that all I am to you?' he demanded, eyes glittering. 'Your stud?'

She cupped his cheeks and rubbed her nose to his. 'Don't be offended. You are a most excellent stud.'

He snatched her wrist and bared his teeth, but then the playfully sensual mood was broken by her phone ringing.

He kissed her. 'Ignore it.'

'I can't.' Flora's phone was on silent so only her emergency contacts could get through,

Alejandro, Sinead and her brother. Alejandro was on top of her, Sinead was in her room adjoining the nursery, so the caller could only be Justin, who usually waited for her to call him when she wasn't with Alejandro.

Wriggling out from under Alejandro, she scrambled to her bedside table to answer it. Her worries that something was wrong were quickly dispelled and she ended the call inordinately proud of her big brother for all the effort he was making with the wreckage of his life, but apprehensive too for what Alejandro's reaction to her brother's intrusion would be.

He'd sat himself back propped against the headboard. All his former playfulness had gone. His arms were folded across his chest, the expression on his face the one he always got whenever the ghost of her brother appeared before them.

Her heart sank.

Would he ever forgive him or was this how it was going to be for the rest of her life, the two men she loved the most estranged for ever?

It didn't have to be like this.

Taking a deep breath for resolve, Flora shuffled over and sat in front of him, crossed her legs and took hold of his hand.

Looking him steadily in the eye, she said, 'Today it has been exactly fifteen months since Justin last gambled.' Exactly fifteen months since Alejandro lured him to Monte Cleure on a business pretext and promptly had him arrested.

His already tight features looked as if they could snap.

'He goes to Gamblers Anonymous meetings three times a week. He has a job as a barista in a coffee shop. He is doing everything he can to be a better man. He will never have the money to pay you back—the money he stole from you was used to pay his gambling debts, as you know—but he is desperate to make amends with you.'

And for all that her brother was turning his life around, the only way he would find peace in himself would be through Alejandro's forgiveness.

'Impossible,' he bit out.

'Why? He spent ten months in a prison cell. He has lost his home, the job he loved, his friends, his self-respect and, most importantly, he has lost you. Is that not punishment enough for you?'

His lips formed in a snarl.

'I love my brother.' She gently massaged his hand, refusing to let his simmering anger divert her. 'I love him and I want Benjamin to get to know and love him too.'

'Over my dead body.'

Flora closed her eyes and took a deep breath. 'I know you miss him.'

He snatched his hand from hers. The words that flew from his mouth were definitely Spanish curses.

'How can you not?' she asked. 'The two of you were as close as brothers.'

'Which makes what he did even worse,' he snapped, throwing the sheets off his lap and climbing off the bed.

'From your perspective, yes.'

'He should have come to me when he first got into trouble.'

'Agreed, but you have to remember his state of mind. All those years he'd known you and you were the golden boy. You had the money, the fame, the first pick of the women... He hero-worshipped you and couldn't bear to tell you how badly he'd screwed up.'

'Yes, he was so worried about losing my respect that he stole my money instead.' He was pacing the floor, clearly agitated.

Was his agitation because she was getting through to him?

She could only hope.

'He stole it stupidly thinking he'd be able to win it all back before you noticed. *That's* how out of his mind he was. Please, I am begging you, let him say his piece to you, and see if you can move on and forgive him. Please, for Benjamin's sake if not for mine or his, and for your sake too—'

'Enough!' he roared, spinning around to face her.

Flora reared back, more shocked at the rage on his face than the fury in his voice.

It had been a long time since she'd seen such anger from him and it hurt her heart to see it.

Visibly composing himself, Alejandro took a deep breath and gritted his teeth. 'I have made my feelings on the subject perfectly clear and I will hear no more about it, and I will thank you to keep the promise you made and keep my son away from him.'

Then he took four paces, snatched his robe off the hook on the bedroom door and, without looking back at her, walked out of their room.

Flora had no idea what time Alejandro came back to bed. He simply slid under the covers and turned his back to her.

He'd never done that before.

She drifted in and out of sleep, the wretchedness in her belly too strong for her to settle.

Since they'd become lovers, they'd bickered but never argued. Not like that. Alejandro had never raised his voice to her.

She just wanted her family to be together again, for her husband and her brother to be friends as they used to be and for her son to know his uncle. She would exchange all the wealth and trappings if she could have that.

All she could hope was that, once his anger faded, Alejandro would think on what she'd said.

It was for his sake too that she wanted

bridges to be built. He missed her brother. She was as certain of that as she was certain of her love for him.

The sound of metal wheels rolling over the oak floor woke her with a snap from the latest doze she'd fallen into.

The room was dusky, the early morning sun still rising.

Alejandro was showered, groomed and dressed in a business suit, suitcase and briefcase in hand, ready for his trip to Paris.

'I am going now,' he said stiffly.

Flora's stomach lurched miserably. His anger didn't seem to have faded a jot.

'Safe travels,' she whispered as she always did.

His chest rose and then he inclined his head and left the room.

For the first time since they'd become lovers, he left for a business trip without kissing her goodbye.

CHAPTER TWELVE

I<small>T WAS LOOKING</small> to be another beautiful early autumn day in Barcelona. Flora was glad that she'd arranged to meet Camila for an early coffee. It meant she could walk there. Hopefully the fresh air would do some good in clearing her head. If it was too hot when they were done, she'd get her driver to collect her.

She checked her phone. Still no communication from Alejandro. He hadn't messaged to let her know he'd arrived in Paris safely—although he had responded to her message asking if he'd got there okay with a simple yes—or called to wish her a goodnight.

The longer his silence went on, the angrier she could feel herself becoming at his stubbornness, so she took a handful of deep breaths for some zen before putting Benjamin in his pram and calling out to Madeline to let her know she was leaving. She got a cheerful shout back.

Things had changed dramatically between Flora and the staff. It was as Alejandro had suggested, although she didn't think the change in their demeanour towards her was entirely down to them sharing a bed but more to do with them being a proper couple and the respect he showed towards her. Respect begat respect. Flora was the master's wife and they now treated her as such.

Before opening the door, she checked her phone again. Still nothing.

Her bodyguards were waiting for her on the doorstep. One carried the pram down as if it weighed nothing more than a bunch of flowers. They still spoke in grunts to her but she now suspected that was because grunts were their language.

Before they reached the gate, her phone pinged. It was a message from Sinead who'd taken the week off, saying her flight had landed.

Flora smiled, pleased to know her son's nanny was safe and well. She was careful not to overstep their professional relationship but Sinead was such a sunny presence that it was impossible not to care about her.

She returned the message with a smiley emoji and put her phone back in her bag just as the gate opened.

A swarm of journalists was waiting for her.

She barely had time to draw breath before she was enveloped in a cacophony of noise as questions were hurled at her and cameras were thrust in her and Benjamin's faces.

Her bodyguards sprang into action. Within seconds they were standing in front of the pram, not allowing the gathered press to step even a millimetre over the threshold of Alejandro's land.

Flora backed away, then turned the pram around and raced a screaming Benjamin back to the villa.

The front door flung open before she reached the steps. Madeline hurried down and helped her carry the pram indoors.

'What's going on?' Flora asked as she lifted her distraught son into her arms. Heavens, she was shaking.

'I not know.' Madeline's obvious worry

only made Flora's nerves more shot. 'Security not see them. Must have hidden.'

Flora swallowed and nodded her understanding. The gate opened onto a wide pathway. The road lined one side, huge trees the other. It would have been easy for the press to keep out of sight of the security cameras until the gates opened and then ambush her.

The house phone rang. Madeline hurried off to answer it.

Holding Benjamin securely with one arm, Flora dug into her bag with her free hand and grabbed her phone, using the voice activation to call Alejandro.

It went straight to voicemail.

Speaking over Benjamin's sobs, she said, 'Ramos, it's me. Something's going on. The press have just ambushed me. I hope everything's okay your end. Call me back as soon as you can.'

The house phone was ringing again.

Flora carried her son into the main living room and sat with him on one of the velvet sofas, trying her best to soothe him, trying not to let her imagination run riot as to why the press would be back when they'd not been anywhere near the villa in months, or worry why the house phone was ringing for a third time.

Once Benjamin had calmed down, Flora called Camila.

'I was just about to call you,' Camila said. 'Are you okay?'

'I think so. I couldn't leave the villa because of the press. What is going *on*?'

She sensed the other woman's hesitation.

'Camila?'

'Have you not looked at any gossip site today?'

'No.' She never did. Not since those pictures of her brother and Alejandro on Alejandro's yacht with all those beautiful women. That had cured her of seeking out his name.

Madeline appeared, pale faced.

'Hold on a minute,' Flora said to Camila before addressing the housekeeper. 'What's wrong?'

'Do I have agreement to pull telephone from…?' As she mimed disconnecting it, it rang again.

'Who keeps calling?'

Madeline made a rude sign that signified it was the press.

'Okay,' Flora agreed, then returned to her call with Camila. 'What's on the gossip sites I should know about?'

'I am sure it doesn't mean anything.' Her friend sounded genuinely distressed.

'What?'

'Alejandro.'

'What about him?'

'He was photographed going into Aimee's apartment last night.'

Flora paced her bedroom.

She'd tried calling Alejandro again a number of times but with the same result.

Her phone vibrated in her hand. She swiped and stuck it to her ear. 'Hello?'

'Hi, Flora, it's Eloise Jameson from the *Daily*—'

Flora swiped again and threw the phone on the floor as if it had scalded her.

She pinched the bridge of her nose and fought back tears. She felt under siege. And alone. Very alone. As if she were in the midst of a horror story. Or a nightmare.

She took a deep breath to try to calm herself before picking her phone up. There was a nice new hairline crack on the screen but it seemed to be working fine. It rang in her hand and she just managed to stop herself from dropping it. Not recognising the number, she refused the call, then diverted all calls to voicemail and fired a message to Alejandro asking him to message her. Only then did she finally pluck up the courage to do a search of his name.

The first thing that came up on her feed was a salacious headline. Swallowing hard to keep the bile at bay, she clicked on the link and was confronted with a set of pictures of her husband. The first had him looking over his shoulder as he approached a doorway. The second had him unlocking the door with his own key. The third had him stepping over the threshold. The fourth was an older picture of Alejandro and Aimee leaving through that door together, used as a comparison to show the reader it was the same apartment building.

Alejandro's beard gave no room for doubt

that the first three pictures were recent, taken after they'd become lovers again.

She couldn't hold it back any longer. Running to the bathroom, she vomited until her stomach was empty.

Benjamin was finally asleep. The day had unsettled him enormously and he'd been as fractious as when he was teething. For now, though, Flora's beautiful boy was calm and hopefully dreaming lovely thoughts in the cot she'd bought for him when she'd been six months pregnant and expecting to raise him alone in London.

Closing the bedroom door softly behind her, she sank slowly to the floor, put the baby monitor on the carpet, and hugged her knees to her chest.

Once she'd emptied her stomach of all its contents, the only thing she could think of was escape. Luck had shined on her. She'd managed to book herself and Benjamin onto the next flight to London.

Ignoring Madeline's protests and the ashen faces of the other household staff, she'd ordered her driver to take her and Benjamin to the airport and within two hours of booking the return flight had been in the air.

Barely twelve hours had passed since the villa's gates had opened and her world had imploded.

She'd spent the day fighting to keep her demons at bay for Benjamin's sake and it had exhausted her. She felt so hollow, as if her heart had been carved out of her.

The stairs creaked. Justin appeared at the top of them and sat beside her.

After a long period of silence he sighed and ran his fingers through his hair. 'He'll go mad when he knows you've brought his son here.'

Flora had already explained everything that had happened these last two days. Justin had listened without speaking, taking it all in.

'I know, but where else could I go?' Who else could she turn to but the rock who'd always been there for her?

There was another long silence before he said, 'Let's hope he sees it like that. And for what it's worth, I don't believe he'd cheat on you.'

'Really?'

He nodded.

'I want to believe that too,' she whispered.

'Look, he's an unforgiving bastard but he's never been a cheat, and he's liked you for a long time. Do you really think I'd have encouraged you with him otherwise?'

She remembered when she'd finally plucked up the courage to tell Justin she was pregnant with Alejandro's child and that Alejandro had cut her off. He'd said nothing, just hung his head in his hands, his devastation obvious. Their marriage had been like a weight off his shoulders. She'd assumed that was because the threat of prison and all the financial burden had been taken care of. Justin had been in such a bad place that she'd taken great pains to hide the blackmail aspect of it and make it sound like marriage to Alejandro was what she wanted too. She hadn't wanted to add to her brother's guilt.

'Are you serious? Did you *want* us to get together?'

He suddenly smiled. 'I'll be honest with you, Flo. I thought he had no chance with you. Not the way you hated him. But I always knew that if he won you round, he'd look after you. You're my sister and our mother's daughter. There was no way he'd have shown an interest if he wasn't serious about you.'

Flora hugged her knees even more tightly. She desperately wanted to believe Alejandro hadn't cheated on her. Desperately wanted to believe that history wasn't repeating itself. But those pictures of him entering Aimee's apartment…all those fears she'd had before, it turned out they hadn't gone, had simply been buried under the bliss of what they'd found together and now they had reared back up; her worst nightmare coming viciously to life.

The last two months had been so good between them that it hadn't even occurred to her to worry about him being in Paris when she *knew* that was where his old mistress lived.

Justin nudged her. 'Get you a drink?'

She tried to smile and managed a nod.

Her return flight was in two days. She would get home around the same time as Alejandro. She would sit down with him and confront him over the pictures. She knew him well enough that she would know if he was lying to her.

She'd never known him to lie, she thought starkly. Or cheat.

What was she supposed to do if he *had* cheated? She couldn't leave him or he'd launch the prosecution against Justin again, and, while she had enough money saved to form a strong defence for him, there was no way Justin would avoid serving prison time.

If Alejandro hadn't cheated, she was in no position to demand future fidelity from him, she thought miserably. No position to demand *anything* from him.

It just went to prove that without Alejandro's love, their marriage was a house built of sand. One hit of a wave and it would come crashing down.

In the kitchen, she found she'd forgotten to switch the plug on when charging her phone earlier after the battery had drained. She sighed and turned it on, then waited for enough charge to go through it to bring it back to life.

Nausea sloshed in her belly. Had Alejandro finally tried to make contact?

Or would she still be met with a wall of silence from him?

'Lemonade in your wine?' Justin asked.

'Yes, please.'

'Fancy watching a film?'

Life flickered on the screen of her phone.

She tried another unsuccessful smile. 'You choose something. I'll join you in a minute.'

Her screen showed she had twenty-four missed calls, eleven voicemails and eighteen text messages.

She clicked on the call icon and her heart jumped. The last missed call had come from Alejandro. He'd tried calling her seven times. The others were from Camila, a couple of her old English friends and numbers she didn't recognise. Alejandro was responsible for only one of the text messages, a short, Call me back as soon as you can.

She went into her voicemail. The first three were messages from the soulless journalists who'd upset her baby so much. The fourth was from Alejandro and her heart clattered to hear his deep voice speak her name into her ear. Before she could hear the rest of it, a loud rap on the front door made her jump.

Some sixth sense kicked in and, her blood turning to ice, she knew immediately who the visitor was.

Justin reached the door before Flora had passed the kitchen threshold. He swung it open and instantly stilled.

Alejandro loomed menacingly in the doorway, still in a work suit despite the late hour, a head taller than her brother. His eyes zoomed over Justin's head and locked onto hers.

Barely a second elapsed before his gaze left her, but the fury in the dark depths was strong enough to land like a punch.

With a withering stare at Justin, he said, 'I am here to speak to my wife. Your presence is not welcome. Leave.'

Justin darted his gaze to Flora. She swallowed hard then nodded. His presence could only make matters worse.

He grabbed his jacket off the coat rack, mimed a 'call me' gesture at Flora, and slipped out of the door.

The atmosphere in the narrow house turned

frigid. Flora rubbed her arms for warmth then pressed a hand to her chest in an effort to temper the loud thuds of her heart.

An age passed with Alejandro's coldly furious stare on her before he spoke. 'Where is my son?'

'Sleeping,' she whispered.

His shoulders rose slowly in a deep inhalation. 'Then let us speak where we will not disturb him.'

Somehow she managed to force her shaking legs into the kitchen, take hold of the baby monitor, and then open the integral door that led into the garage she'd had converted into a studio for her work when she'd bought the house two years ago.

Alejandro's eyes flickered around, no doubt taking it all in.

He'd never been in her home before. She'd never invited him.

Flora's studio was a small space but worked perfectly for her. She had a large table at one end with stacks of her designs, her sewing machine and other paraphernalia on it, and wide shelves filled with rolls of fabric and fat rolls of thread lining the walls either side of it. On the other side was a small sofa she often sat on when curled up hand-stitching.

She sat on her desk chair, leaving the sofa for him.

He hooked an ankle to a thigh and contemplated her with the imperious expression that took her back seven months to the day he'd blackmailed her, married her and then been the most supportive birthing partner a woman could have. The day he'd shown the best and the worst of himself.

'Let's get this over with, shall we?' she said shakily, unable to bear the silence any longer. 'I'm sorry for bringing Benjamin to London but I needed to escape Barcelona for a couple of days. I couldn't leave him behind because Sinead's on holiday.'

Barely a muscle flickered on his face. 'Why didn't you wait for me to call you back?'

'I waited two hours. Why didn't you answer my calls and messages?'

He unhooked his ankle, rested his palms on his thighs and stared her right in her eye. 'One of my casino managers had a heart attack during our breakfast meeting.'

The shock of his answer made her gasp.

'I performed CPR while we waited for the paramedics to arrive, then travelled with him to the hospital. His wife met us there. I stayed with her until the surgeon finished operating on him because she was in no state to be left alone.' Something dark flashed in his eyes. 'I don't suppose you can imagine it, but she was distraught. I didn't think it right to check my messages while she was out of her mind with fear that she would never see her husband again.'

Flora covered her face then dragged her fingers down it, utterly wretched for the poor man but even more so for his wife. She could hardly bring herself to imagine the agony she must have gone through knowing the life of the man she loved was hanging in the balance.

'How is he?' she asked hoarsely.

'Stable.'

'You saved his life?'

'The doctors saved his life,' he corrected before his lips curled. 'When I left the hospital I saw all your messages but I could not get hold of you. I spoke to Madeline, who filled me in on what had happened and told me that not only had you left the country and flown to England but that you had taken my son with you.'

His voice dripped with barely concealed fury.

Flora held his stare and swallowed back a swell of nausea. 'You were at her apartment last night.'

'*My* apartment,' he corrected. 'I kicked Aimee out after that little stunt she pulled for the paparazzi when Benjamin was born. I am selling it. I've had it refurbished and wanted to check the workmanship before I give the go-ahead to put it on the market.'

The relief that should have come at this explanation refused to form. Her heart was beating too fast for relief. It was Alejandro's demeanour. The iciness in it. 'Why didn't you tell me any of this?'

'I didn't want to upset you. I know you hate my past. I was going to sell the apartment and then that would be it—the last link of any woman in my past gone. You know why I was doing that?'

She shook her head.

'For you.' He smiled. It was the coldest

smile she'd ever received. 'And you assumed I was cheating on you, didn't you?'

'I didn't know what to think.'

'Yes, you did. At the first sign of trouble, you assumed the worst of me and took my son and ran away from me, and ran away to the one man you knew I didn't want Benjamin anywhere near.'

'It wasn't like that. I didn't run away from you. I ran from the situation.'

His disbelieving icy stare made the knots in her stomach tighten. 'The press, the pictures...' She took a deep breath, trying her hardest to speak coherently. 'We never made the usual promises married couples make. You never promised to be faithful—if you had, I would have known there was more to those photos than what the press were implying because I know you don't lie or make false promises, but it was understood that you would still take lovers if you wished.'

'Understood by you. Not me. Just because your jealousy made you act perversely and give your blessing for me to have affairs did not mean I would act on it, and I cannot believe you think so little of me that you think

I would leave your bed in the morning and be in another woman's bed that same night… No, actually, I can believe it.' Alejandro's eyes glittered, his handsome features contorting into bitterness. 'You think all men are cheats.'

'No!' Flora bowed her head and let her hair fall like a stream over her face.

The beats of her heart had become the beats of doom.

'I was *scared*. You left on an argument and without kissing me goodbye. You didn't call to wish me goodnight, and then the press ambushed me and I saw those pictures and I couldn't get hold of you and all I could think was that I needed to escape to somewhere safe.'

'You described yourself as an expert on men's infidelities,' he said flatly. 'You said you didn't think a leopard could change its spots. Isn't this what you've been waiting for? Have I made you so damn miserable that you've been waiting for the first opportunity to leave me?'

'Don't be so ridiculous. I couldn't leave you even if I wanted to!' she cried, stung that he could think such a thing after everything they'd shared.

For a long time he just stared at her, firm lips tightening, the darkness in his eyes turning into granite. 'So you do want to leave me?'

'I didn't say that! I said I couldn't leave you *even* if I wanted to, and I can't, can I? Not with the threat of you reopening my brother's prosecution hanging over my head.'

Slowly, he lifted his hands from his lap and placed them behind his neck, his granite eyes not leaving her face. Then he lifted his chin and said, 'If I took that threat away and asked you to choose between me and your brother, who would win?'

'I…' She shook her head, caught off-guard.

'It is a simple question, Flora. Me or him. Because it is a choice you have to make if our marriage is to continue.'

She stared at him. Was he really saying what she thought he was saying? He wouldn't. No. She must be misunderstanding him.

'I need to know your loyalty is with me, so make your choice. Him or me.'

Dear God, he was being serious.

'Do you *want* me to hate you?' she managed to choke.

'I want a wife who I can trust. Last chance. Him or me. Make your choice and make it now or I will take your silence as a choice for him.'

Her head was spinning. It wasn't possible that he could make such a cruel ultimatum. 'It's an impossible choice. How am I supposed to choose between you? *I can't.*'

He got to his feet and wiped the sleeves of his jacket. It wasn't just his eyes that were like granite. His features were the hardest she had ever seen them, set like stone.

'Then I have my answer. You can consider our marriage over.'

The dizziness that rent through her was so strong Flora had to grab hold of her desk to stop herself falling off her chair.

Almost too late, her eyes focused through the swimming haze in her brain to see Alejandro was heading for the studio door, and her legs suddenly propelled her to her feet, and she threw herself in front of him, blocking his exit.

'You are not seriously going to do this, are you?'

He looked over her head. 'Get out of my way.'

'Don't,' she beseeched, grabbing his arm. Flora had sensed Alejandro hardening his heart against her from the moment he arrived but now she feared he had shut it down completely. 'Please, Alejandro, I know you're angry with me but you don't have to do this. Please, we can—'

His mouth formed a snarl. '*Now* you call me by my name? Now? When you have spent *months* refusing?' He covered her hand and prised her fingers off his arm, face right in front of hers, eyeball to eyeball. 'There is no "we" and never has been. You share my bed but give no more. You don't care when I leave, you never ask to travel with me. You have no loyalty to me. I did everything in my power to make you happy but the only thing you wanted me for was sex. To you, I'm just your *stud*. Now get out of my way.'

CHAPTER THIRTEEN

'I SAID, GET out of my way,' Alejandro said coldly when she didn't move, his gaze now fixed over her head.

'No.' Needing to douse the rising panic, Flora folded her shaking arms tightly over her chest, protecting her thumping heart from flying out of her ribs. 'I'll move when you've listened to what I have to say.'

His tone was contemptuous. 'There is nothing you have to say that I want to hear.'

'I don't care if you want to hear it, I'm going to say it and then you can go on your merry way and leave me to pick up the wreckage, just as you did last time.'

That made him look at her.

'You cut me out so effectively I had to show you I was pregnant with your child in a public forum. I went through the whole pregnancy alone. That was a wreckage of your making, and I had no one. I couldn't turn to my brother for help because he was fighting for his liberty.'

'A consequence of his own actions,' he corrected harshly.

'He was your best friend. You knew his theft was completely out of character. You knew how much Mum's death had screwed with his head—'

'I told you before, do not use your mother's death as an excuse for him.'

'Why not when you use your mother's death as an excuse for your own despicable behaviour?'

The look on his face could have turned lava to ice. 'How dare you?'

Flora was in no mood to be intimidated. This day had been a roller coaster of emotions, a fitting end, she thought bitterly, for a marriage that had started life on its own emotional roller coaster of a day. 'You threw away thirteen years of friendship over one mistake. Justin abused your trust but he hurt you too, but you can't bring yourself to admit that, can you, not the great Alejandro Ramos who's unable to be hurt and isn't afraid of anything? Instead of admitting that he hurt you, you packed more ice around your heart and sought vengeance, and now you're doing the same thing to me, and not for the first time—you read my brother's message and assumed what it meant, and now you're preparing to cut me out again.'

Alejandro was breathing heavily through his nose, his jaw clenched, his gaze unseeing.

'You blackmailed me into this marriage. Or do you forget that? You forced it on me, but despite it all, I tried, for Benjamin's sake, and because you showed the most wonderful side to yourself when he was born...' She gritted her teeth and took a deep breath. 'I knew the danger you posed to my heart and protecting it against you is a battle I've fought every single day of our marriage. It's a battle I've fought for years.'

She thought she caught a flicker in his distant, unseeing gaze.

Dropping her voice, she said, 'That weekend when you came back to Oxford early because your dad had gone off to Martinique... I saw you naked. Just a glimpse through the gap in my bedroom door. I was thirteen years old.'

His eyes suddenly regained their focus and widened in shock.

'You woke something in me,' she confessed, 'and I haven't looked at another man since. I have spent over ten years insanely jealous of the women in your life and comparing myself to them. The only reason I gave you my blessing to have affairs was because of my stupid pride—I was *terrified* you'd see how deeply my feelings for you ran. I've been running from them for *years*. All I have ever known is men who cheat and lie and discard women when the next pretty thing comes along… You knocked my barriers down, but I got too close, didn't I? That's what this is all about, isn't it? I got close enough to hurt you.'

His throat moved and he shook his head. For a short moment she thought he was going to say something but then the moment was gone.

Flora filled her lungs with air and her heart with resolve. 'It *is* the truth. You're not incapable of being hurt like you pretend to yourself. You're scared of it. You have the most wonderful side to you, Alejandro. You're fun and considerate and affectionate and incredibly loving, but the second someone hurts you, you shut down. You twist the pain of their hurt into anger and strike back.

'You lost the most precious person in your life far too young but pain and hurt are facts of life. Grief is too. There were days I thought the pain of losing my mum would kill me. That pain was the price I paid for loving her, but I wouldn't trade a single day of her life to have erased that pain. You were a child when you went through that grief and I get why you shut down emotionally from it, but you're an adult now, with a child of your own. What are you going to do when Benjamin hurts you? Because one day he will. Are you going to turn that pain into anger and strike back at him? Will you shut him out of your heart too? Your own flesh and blood?'

The baby monitor suddenly came to life. The sound of their son's cries cut through the toxic atmosphere swirling around them.

Feeling sick, Flora stepped forwards and placed a hand on Alejandro's frozen chest.

Staring hard into his eyes, she said, 'When you're old and lonely and thinking back on our marriage, remember you were the one who threw us away. Despite all the odds, you did make me happy; very happy. I fell in love with you and I think a part of you fell in love with me too. We could have had something good but you were too scared to take it. You gave me the cruellest ultimatum you could and you made it because you knew I would never turn my back on my brother. You *wanted* this outcome and, in all honesty, I'm glad of it. Anyone who can make an ultimatum like that and try to force someone to give up someone who means so much to them doesn't deserve love, and you don't deserve mine. Now, I'm going to see to our son. You can see yourself out.'

And then, she turned around, opened her studio door, and walked away from him.

Benjamin's bright red cheeks and high-pitched wails told Flora he was teething again. Her battered heart ached for him. Every time she put him down, he started crying again and she ended up settling with him on her bed and letting him fall asleep in her arms. A good hour passed before she remembered to message her brother and tell him he was safe to come home.

A short while later there was a tap on her bedroom door and her brother's worried face emerged.

She swallowed hard and shook her head.

He closed his eyes briefly before padding over to perch on the side of her bed. 'I'm sorry,' he whispered.

A tear fell down her cheek. 'So am I.'

He kissed the top of her head and left the room, closing the door softly behind him.

Flora kept a tight grip on the swell of emotions battering her until she put Benjamin back in his cot beside her bed and he stayed in peaceful sleep. Only then did she crawl under her bedsheets and sob until her throat was raw and her insides battered and bruised.

Justin was already in the kitchen when Flora carried Benjamin down for his breakfast.

'You look exhausted,' he observed, taking Benjamin from her and putting him in his high chair.

'Thank you.' She tried to sound bright but her vocal cords obeyed only to a 'listless' level. It had been the longest night of her life. Every time she'd drifted into sleep she'd had dreams of Alejandro walking past her in the Monte Cleure court, looking straight through her, not hearing her pleas, Flora a ghost he could not see. She'd snapped herself awake from all of them, frozen in her chest and her face soaked in tears.

'Why don't I take him out for a walk?' Justin said once she'd fed Benjamin his cereal and given him his bottle of milk. 'You go back to bed.'

'I don't need—'

'Yes, you do. Go and get his change bag for me and I'll take him to the park.'

Oh, but she felt wretched. She hadn't told Justin that the prosecution against him would be reopened…although, now she thought about it, she didn't remember Alejandro mentioning it, but it must be a given…and she opened her mouth to deliver the heartbreaking news, but what came out was, 'Are you sure?'

'He's my nephew. Of course I'm sure.'

She closed her eyes and smiled wanly in thanks.

Let her brother spend some time with his nephew in the fresh air before she gave him the news that would destroy his life again.

Soon, Benjamin was secure in the pram that had been sat in the understairs cupboard since she'd bought it all that time ago, and she was kissing them both goodbye.

The house felt so silent without them.

Dragging her weary legs back to the kitchen to get herself a glass of water, Flora found herself staring at her studio door. The space she'd created, her happy place, now tainted for ever.

Would she ever be able to enter her studio without thinking of him and remembering how he'd ripped the heart out of her?

She couldn't take any pleasure at getting the last word in or from the image of his ashen face when she'd told him to let himself out.

Her words had wounded him, she was sure of it, and, like a wounded animal, it would only make him more dangerous. She should be frightened at where this could lead but her heart refused to accept how far he would go. She didn't believe for a second he would ever try to take Benjamin from her, not even out of vengeance… He hadn't mentioned custody either.

She didn't have the strength right then to pray she wasn't mistaken in this, not when her heart was so bruised with grief at how it had ended between them, because that was what it felt like. Grief.

But she had to be strong. She had her baby to think of and her brother's future to deal with and could not afford the luxury of wallowing over a man who, however happy he had made her, didn't deserve her love.

Rubbing away the fresh tears that had let loose, she was filled with resolve and she marched to her studio door and threw it open…and almost screamed when she saw the figure on the sofa, doubled over, head slumped forwards on his lap, hands clutching his dark hair.

Certain she was hallucinating, Flora blinked a number of times.

'Alejandro?' she whispered.

Slowly, the head lifted.

She covered her mouth in horror. The beautiful, meltingly dark eyes were puffy and bloodshot.

Frightened, she took a tentative step towards him.

A contortion of emotions danced over his haggard face. He held out a hand to her. It was shaking.

She took another step and touched the tips of her fingers to his. He sank to his knees and wrapped his arms around her, holding her so tightly all the breath was pushed from her lungs.

'I'm sorry, I'm sorry,' he sobbed into her breasts. 'So sorry.'

Utterly thrown, her heart ripping at the animalistic sounds coming from this most arrogant and prideful of men, Flora instinctively cradled him tightly and kissed the top of his head.

When the shudders wracking his powerful body abated, sense came back to her and she let go of him, but before she could step away from his hold, he lifted his head to stare into her eyes. 'I...'

He swallowed and squeezed his eyes shut.

Then he took a long breath before fixing his desolate gaze back on her.

'I tried to go,' he said hoarsely. 'But I couldn't. I couldn't make my body leave. I couldn't stop the thoughts...' He grimaced tightly and loosened an arm from around her waist to tap the side of his head. 'So many thoughts. Memories. The people I have cut from my life. I thought life is too short to give second chances. Not everyone deserves a second chance. Hillier didn't but he deserved the chance to make amends. I denied him that. Worse... I used him as a weapon to get to you.'

At her shocked stare, he smiled grimly. 'I think...' He swallowed again and took her hands in his.

'Let me start from the beginning because it all starts with you. *Querida*, I have been in love with you for years. Your twenty-first birthday, that's when I fell for you. I looked at you and what I felt was like nothing before it. Hillier's little sister all grown up and so beautiful it hurt my heart. One dance was all you let me have. You trembled the whole time.' He pressed her hand to his chest.

She could feel the strong thuds of his heart against it. 'I could feel your heart beating against me like a little hummingbird... And then you ran away like a frightened mouse.'

Flora's heart was beating like a hummingbird now.

Was she dreaming? Had she not actually woken up at all?

Alejandro only opened himself up to her in her dreams.

The eyes gazing into hers were swirling with more emotion than she'd ever seen in her dreams.

'After that night, I couldn't get you from my mind,' he whispered. 'For months I tried to entice you to me. I would get your brother to invite you to functions with us but you refused them all, apart from my birthday party but you ran away again.' Sadness shadowed his face. 'And then your mother's condition deteriorated when things had been so hopeful. When I visited... I had so much admiration for the way you cared for her. You were like an angel watching over her.' He smiled wistfully. 'An angel making jokes that kept a smile on your mother's face until the end.

Hiding your pain for her sake but never hiding your love. And you have so much love in you, *querida*.

'When she died, everything changed. The house I had always been welcome in was sold and for a year I saw nothing of you... and then you turned up at my home a week after your brother's arrest...' He shook his head, self-disgust emanating off him like a wave. 'I knew you would come to me to save him. Believe me, please, it was not done on a conscious level, but something was driving me to take the actions I did against him and when I look back I can see that was you. I knew you would come to me.'

She *must* be dreaming...

'That night with you blew my mind. To know I was your first...' He closed his eyes and inhaled deeply before locking his stare back to hers. 'Turning my back on you is the cruellest thing I have ever done and I do not seek your forgiveness. What I did to you was unforgivable. That night...how you looked at me the next morning... I had dreamt of you looking at me like that for so long. But I am everything you accused me of being.

Scared of feelings. Like a child trapped in a man's body.

'I went to great lengths to stop you making contact with me again. I told myself it was because I hated you for using me and for snubbing me all those years and only wanting me so you could save him, but it was because, that night, you made me feel too much. You are my one weakness, *querida*. My Achilles heel. And for all my efforts, I could not stop thinking of you. You were a plague in my head I had no cure for.' He inhaled deeply and brushed his lips as lightly as a feather over the tips of her fingers. 'I was your first and you were my last. There has been no one but you since that night.'

Flora's hummingbird heart jumped into her throat. It wasn't just the words he was saying but how he was saying them, the fluency of his English more jumbled, his accent more pronounced. Agony and sincerity vibrated in every syllable.

'I didn't sleep for weeks before the court case. I knew you would be there and I would see you again and that you would hate me… Deservedly.' He inhaled through his nose. 'I had much guilt. Much vengeance but much guilt too. I had pushed the situation with your brother so far—too far—and my conscience was not happy with me. I had nightmares of him as an old man in jail. You were in those dreams too, crying and pleading with me.

'You carrying my child was the dream I never knew I had come true. I could end the prosecution of your brother without losing face but, more importantly, I had the means to tie you to me for ever, and I took it. I wish I could call it madness, the thing that gripped me and forced you to marry me, but that would be kind. It was monstrous. *I* was monstrous. All night I have been going over that day and asking myself what possessed me to do that to you and I will not insult your intelligence by calling it love. I was in love with you but my actions were not those of a man in love. They were the actions of a monster. Real love came later. It grew in me. Every day it got deeper, but the demons that have lived with me for so long, they were still there. I tried to forget how our marriage was forged. I tried to forget my actions, but just as it is impossible to forgive my actions, it is impossible to forget them too, and deep down I never believed you could forgive or forget them or love me because of them, so when you fled to England and to your brother...

'*Querida*, that is when I realised just how much power you have over me. The self-protection that has shielded my heart from hurt since I was a child did what it always does.'

He brought her fingers to his mouth again then smiled tightly and released them. Rising, he sat back on the sofa and rubbed the back of his head before looking back at her. 'You were right to call it like packing my heart with ice. I don't know how to be any other way. But I must learn, for Benjamin's sake. I see that.' A small, sad smile played on his lips. 'But I think he will melt the ice like his mother does.'

Alejandro's eyes squeezed shut and his throat moved. His gaze when he opened them was utterly desolate. 'Losing you... how I'm feeling now...is the greatest pain I have ever known and there is nothing I can do to stop it. I have to find a way to live with it and accept it as due punishment. When I leave here, I will have the prosecution file on your brother shredded and I will instruct my lawyer to contact you—give him your terms for the divorce and custody of Benjamin. I will not fight you.' His lips tugged into another small, sad smile. 'You think I had the power in our marriage? *Querida*, you had it all. You have complete power over me, and I want you to know the months of our marriage were the best of my life. You are an incredible woman and I will regret the pain I have caused you until my dying day.'

The pumping of her freshly swelling heart was so strong blood rushed to her head, dizzying her.

She felt as if she'd just been spun a thousand times on a Waltzer.

All this time. All these years.

When Alejandro rose to his feet and bowed his head to her, she followed him with her eyes as he walked stiffly to the door, a thousand thoughts filling her head.

All this time…

Snapshots came to her, one after the other, a picture reel of images.

That look between them on her twenty-first birthday. The thrills and terror to be held in his arms when they danced.

The joy on his face when he'd spotted her at his party. The concern when she'd fled so early from it.

The tenderness and compassion in his eyes at her mother's funeral.

The hunger and need etched on his face the moment before their lips fused together that first time.

The icy fury in his eyes in the court waiting room. The triumph when she agreed to marry him. The flash of panic when he realised the birth was imminent.

The tender encouragement throughout the birth.

The swirl of pride, relief and happiness that had lit his face when he first held their son in his arms.

Love had been there in every one of those images. Love for her.

Hadn't she known it? His feelings for her?

And she'd run and run and run.

She'd been right to run, but not for the reasons she'd told herself. Alejandro would never cheat on her. He would never lie, not consciously. But she'd been right to run because the Alejandro she'd been running from hadn't been capable of fully opening his heart and letting her inside it, not with the monsters that had plagued him for so long.

The monsters he'd just spent a long, lonely night torturing himself over. Admitting them. Banishing them…maybe not for good, but Alejandro's determination meant he would succeed in banishing them completely. He would do it for her and their son.

He loved her. Truly loved her.

And she loved him.

Flora's feelings for him had always been so rabid and greedy and *terrifying*, but as the picture reel faded and her eyes soaked in the proud but broken flesh and blood man who'd just opened his soul up to her, her heart bloomed like a giant rose and for the first time she realised all her fear had gone.

'Wait,' she called out to him as he reached for the door handle.

His back muscles tensed before he slowly turned back around to face her.

'How long do we have to wait for the divorce to go through?' she asked.

'In Monte Cleure, divorce is allowed after a year of marriage,' he said hollowly.

'Is there a separation period?'

He winced but didn't drop his stare. 'No.'

'So we can divorce in five months' time?'

He inclined his head curtly.

'And then can we remarry immediately after?'

He froze.

'But somewhere nicer than Monte Cleure,' she added. 'And in a church. And I'd like to wear a wedding dress. And have a honeymoon. Do it all properly.'

His mouth moved but nothing came out.

'And I suppose I'll have to let my dad give me away. Unless you agree that Justin can do it?'

Flora held her breath while she waited for him to respond.

Alejandro attempted to clear his throat a number of times. He shook his head. 'No. Your father will have to do it. Hillier will be my best man.'

For the longest time nothing more was said. Not verbally. Their eyes though... Flora could feel the emotions flooding Alejandro as vividly as she could feel the emotions flooding her, all warm and joyous and ballooning into her every crevice.

And then he moved.

In three long strides he was hauling her into his arms and holding her tightly enough to squeeze all the air from her lungs again. When his mouth found hers, his kiss was the most passionate and reverential she had ever tasted, leaving her clinging to him weak-kneed with giddiness as much as with need for him.

'I love you,' she said when he finally pulled his mouth from hers to rain kisses over her cheeks. 'I love you so much.'

He cupped her face. 'How?' he asked simply.

She smiled and stroked his cheekbone. 'Because when you're not being a vengeful bastard, you're actually pretty wonderful, and you make me feel *everything*.'

He gazed at her with wonderment. 'You're my life, do you know that?'

Yes, she thought dreamily, she *did* know that. 'And you're mine.'

He kissed her. 'I love you.'
She kissed him back. 'Always.'
'For ever.'

EPILOGUE

THE CATHEDRAL SHONE brightly under the summer sky. With her father's help, Flora got out of the limousine, being careful not to trip over the train of her ivory wedding dress. Camila, dressed in a baby-blue bridesmaid dress, got out of the car behind with Benjamin and her daughter Ava, who were pageboy and flower girl, and somehow managed to herd the two toddlers to the cathedral door to wait for the bridal party's cue to enter. Only Ava reacted to the flash of the paparazzi cameras, cheekily sticking her tongue out while simultaneously waving at them.

Flora's divorce two weeks ago had been front page news in the Spanish tabloids and the top trending item on social media. She was quite sure her subsequent remarriage that day to the same man would beat it for coverage. She might even buy some copies of the papers and magazines herself, for posterity. Something to show the grandkids.

The cue came.

Flora took hold of her dad's arm and planted a kiss to his cheek. He might be a useless, cheating deadbeat but he was still her dad and she now lived in hope that one day he might become less of a cheating deadbeat. If her brother could turn his life around then anyone could.

And there was her brother, right beside the groom, waiting for her. The path to forgiveness had turned out to be surprisingly easy. Alejandro being Alejandro, when he set his mind to something he didn't stop until he achieved it. His mind had been set on finding forgiveness and understanding of his old friend. They would never have the friendship they'd once shared—and Flora wouldn't want them to have that one, thanks very much!—but it was a friendship all the same and for that she was content.

As she walked down the aisle, giving a discreet wave to Louise, Justin's pregnant fiancée, she felt a kick in her belly. It was such a special moment that she stopped and put her hand to her stomach so she could feel it under her palm.

It happened again.

She hurried her movements to Alejandro and, as soon as she was standing beside him, she forgot all propriety and put his hand to her belly so the man she loved could feel their child kick for the first time too.

* * * * *

LET'S TALK

Romance

For exclusive extracts, competitions
and special offers, find us online:

f facebook.com/millsandboon

⊙ @millsandboonuk

🐦 @millsandboon

Or get in touch on 0844 844 1351*

For all the latest titles coming soon,
visit millsandboon.co.uk/nextmonth

*Calls cost 7p per minute plus your phone company's price per
minute access charge

Want even more
ROMANCE?

Join our bookclub today!